Dear Father

Dee Miller

Prairie Sage Books—Prairie Du Sac, WI
ISBN: 978-1-7372955-1-8
Library of Congress Control Number: 2022910058
Title: *Dear Father*
Author: Dee Miller
Digital distribution | 2022
Paperback | 2022

This is a work of fiction. The characters, names, incidents, places, and dialogue are products of the author's imagination, and are not to be construed as real.

Dedication

Thank you to my sons, Joshua and Jesse for being with me on this journey. Your insight and recommendations were invaluable. Your love and support over the years has meant the world to me. I am so proud to call you, my sons.

A special thank you to my readers for your kind words. Your encouragement is the reason *Dear Father* came into existence.

Chapter 1

Riveted to the chair alongside the wrought iron bed, Betty discerned she should do something. She needed to do something, but what? All reason escaped her. Her body would not allow her to move. She remained sitting, immobile with tears cascading downward on her face. She tasted the salt as they trailed across her cheeks and touched her lips. Once the dam burst open, there was no stopping the flow. She'd kept the tears inside too long. Her beloved mother, Anneliese, laid in the bed next to her. She had just taken her last breath. Her mother was too young to die, taken from her far too soon.

Betty, powerless to release the grip she held, peered through her tears, forcing her to look at the still body lying there. She wasn't certain what she expected to see. The expression of serenity on her mother's face stunned her. The pain had at long last ended; not just the pain from the cancer ravaging through her body, but the anguish she encountered throughout her entire existence. Her mother experienced so much loss in her lifetime. Her quest to discover love and find happiness had repeatedly eluded her. Just when it was within her grasp, something invariably happened. Her path constantly taking twists and turns, never catching a break. It was not fair.

Life for Anneliese had never been easy. The challenges, trials and heartaches Anneliese dealt with were unlike any other. It was amazing she hadn't turned into a bitter, nasty person like her mother, Martha, had been. With everything Anneliese had gone through, no one would fault her. Betty was unsure how her mother pulled herself together after every devastating situation, making the best of her life. Betty marveled at how she managed it, but somehow or other, she kept moving forward.

Betty shifted her head, peering around the room. It was the same four walls her grandmother lied when she passed years before. Anneliese moved into the downstairs bedroom after the cancer worsened and she could no longer climb the stairs. Three generations lived together in this big house. Her grandmother, Martha, her mother, Anneliese, and her. Betty grew up an only child. Her mother raising her by herself.

Betty never met her father; did not know who he even was. Rarely did her mother mention him over the years. She'd been unsuccessful in soliciting any information from her, even as she was dying. Betty, hopeful her mother might at last tell her the story of her birth before it was too late, was devastated when it never materialized. She pledged to herself she'd find her father no matter what it took or where he was. She refused to let her family story end here. She needed answers.

Betty felt desolate sitting alone, wishing she had a sibling who could share her grief, someone to call family. She recalled her mother's wish before she died. She asked her to promise she'd break the cycle. To have a house full of offspring. To never raise an only child as she had done. Her mother had also been an only child, making the Doyle lineage almost nonexistent. Betty's desire was to change that, she wanted lots of children. She never wanted a child of hers to grow up alone, so it was an easy promise to make to her dying mother.

A sudden noise in the distance jolted her from her thoughts. Unsure how long she had been sitting there, Betty wondered, *what time is it?* She noticed how cool her mother's hand had become. Her perception was she'd been here longer than it seemed. She urged herself to move. Gently, she unfurled her fingers intertwined with her mother's. It was time. She couldn't remain sitting, pretending it wasn't the worse day of her life.

She forced herself to stand. When she did, she knocked over the chair, causing a banging thump as it struck the floor. Kenneth came charging in. A panic-stricken expression on his face. He raced over to where Betty stood, as she collapsed in his arms. He didn't have time to check out the surrounding scene. His concern was solely for his fiancé.

Her limbs had grown stiff and weak, giving out when she stood. She had been sitting with her mother for days, choosing to not leave her side, needing to be with her. Her mother invariably always taking care of her, now their roles were reversed. She was oblivious to how fragile she became from inactivity and eating little. She was fortunate Kenneth grabbed her as she stumbled.

To keep herself upright, she clung to him, reluctant to let go. As he held her, he glanced over Betty's shoulder. For the first time, recognizing Anneliese was no longer breathing.

"I'm sorry," he said, whispering into her hair.

"It's ok. She is no longer suffering. She has suffered enough."

"Knowing that doesn't make it any easier," he said, trying to console her. "Please, come with me."

He urged her forward, forcing her from the bedroom to the kitchen, leading her to the narrow table that sat in the middle of the room. He pulled out the chair for her to sit, before striding over to the stove, to pour her a cup of coffee. He set the hot beverage in front of her. It had been a while since she'd eaten, so he wanted to offer her something, but he'd wait, knowing she'd refuse, anyway.

Betty picked up her mug, took a sip of the steaming liquid, burning the roof of her mouth. The pain caused her to wince, jarring her back to the present. Her fixation on the burn was a welcome diversion from what had just transpired.

Kenneth, sitting in the opposite chair, held her hand. No words needed to be said. He understood how important Betty's mother was in her life. How much she meant to her. Nothing he said could ease her suffering, yet he wanted her to understand he was there, supporting her. He loved her. They continued sitting together in silence. The only sound heard was her cup clanking against the saucer as the moments passed.

Kenneth, assuring himself she was doing better, patted her hand and stood. He strode over to the telephone, picked up the receiver and dialed. Betty, unable to understand the conversation, sensed who was on the other end. Soon, the funeral home would arrive to take her mother away from the house she lived in her entire life. After making a few other calls, Kenneth came and sat beside her once again. She was doing her best despite her internal struggles.

The sunlight shining through the kitchen window mesmerized Betty. She stared ahead, hearing the birds singing outside. She marveled at how joyful they sounded when she was so miserable. She had to do something; she couldn't just sit here. There were matters requiring her attention.

Before her mother became really ill, they had celebrated her life. It had been a fantastic night, with friends and acquaintances showing up to commemorate her. It made her mother happy to see everyone, and she had enjoyed herself immensely. Now, with her passing, there were other things needing done. It was accomplishing nothing to just sit here.

She reached out to Kenneth and asked. "Kenneth, can you please wait here until they come to take mother away?"

"Of course, whatever you need. I'm here for you."

"There are calls I need to make, and I need to choose an outfit for Mother to wear," she explained.

She quickly interjected, when he gave her a worried look.

"I'm fine. I can handle this. Don't worry."

"Betz, it's ok to be sad. Let yourself cry," Kenneth said.

She adored it when he called her Betz. It was a whole new identity for her.

Betty was my name as a girl. Betz might become my new name, she thought to herself.

Betty took both her hands and placed them on Kenneth's cheeks. She looked directly in his eyes, and struggled with her words, "Thank you. I love and appreciate you, but please understand, I have been grieving since the day we were told the diagnosis. It's true. This is one of the darkest days of my life. My mother has been my entire existence, but she was a person of action. She would not want me sitting here, doing nothing."

Betty grabbed her coffee cup and saucer, carrying them to the kitchen sink. She turned on the faucet, washing them off before placing them back in the cupboard amongst the others. She hurriedly walked to the phone and dialed Pauline's number.

Chapter 2

Pauline hung up the phone, falling to her knees, holding her head in her hands. Her body trembled from her anguished sobs. Her beloved friend just left this world. Though she understood the seriousness of her illness, she had not expected death to come so soon. The call reminding her life was too short.

When Anneliese told her about the cancer, they both cried. They thought they had years to enjoy life, especially since their children were now grown, but the diagnosis changed everything. It wasn't fair. The disease robbed them of time together. Something she'd taken for granted.

They had done many crazy things in their youth. They had been together through both good and hard times. Her friend never had it easy. Yet, despite life's challenges, she knew how to have fun. The time spent together will be forever ingrained in her memory.

My sweet, dear friend. I will miss you.

The news of Anneliese's passing was emotional, but there wasn't time to dwell on her own loss. She was not willing to allow her best friend's daughter handle things on her own. She had to pull herself together. She had to help. Her moment for grieving could wait.

Pauline did not want Betty to see how overwrought the phone call made her. She needed to stay strong for both of them. Pulling herself together, she wandered to the bathroom to check her makeup. There was black underneath her eyes from the mascara and liner she applied that morning, now ruined from the tears she shed. She wet a cloth and swiped both eyes, rubbing gently. She peered closer at the woman in the mirror, unable to recognize herself, touching the fine lines on her face.

When did I become old?

Satisfied she was presentable; she grabbed her keys off the front hall table. She got into her car and drove the route to her beloved friend's house, just as she had many times before. Today was different, her friend would not be there to greet her. She experienced a sudden pang in her heart at the thought. This was going to be difficult.

She placed her foot on the brakes, bringing the vehicle to a stop in front of the familiar house. It was a surreal moment. She wished she were somewhere else, any place other than here.

She checked herself once more in the rear-view mirror, opened the car door and stepped out on the pavement.

I can do this.

Chapter 3

After hanging up the phone with Pauline, the next phone call Betty made was to her best friend, Evelyn. The two of them had known each other since grade school. They became fast friends when Evelyn stood up to the bullies that called her names for being illegitimate, not having a father. Their friendship began that day and continued throughout their lives. They were always there for each other.

When Evelyn answered the phone, Betty could not help but let out a sob. Betty could hardly get the words out. Evelyn knew immediately what happened, and promised she'd be right there.

Pauline and Evelyn arrived at the Doyle home at the same time. As they reached the massive front porch, they looked at one another with sadness in their eyes. Pauline reached out and gave Evelyn's hand a squeeze. They were here for Betty. There was no doubt she needed them both.

They found Betty sitting on the bed in her mother's upstairs bedroom, staring at the closet. When she saw the two women, tears gushed up in her eyes. They reached for her, and she welcomed the arms that engulfed her.

"I am so sorry for your loss." They spoke in unison.

"I hoped I was ready for this," she sobbed. "I thought since she was expected to die; I'd not react this way. It's just so hard to accept she's gone."

"Loss is never easy," Pauline said in a soothing voice. "No one can prepare themselves for how they will behave."

"Give yourself a break," Evelyn gently scolded. "You just lost your mother, your friend, your family."

"Thank you both for being here. I appreciate it more than you know."

Betty pulled herself from the group hug. "I need your help in selecting an outfit for Mother. I thought I could do it myself, but when I saw all of her lovely clothes, I just couldn't bring myself to do it."

An idea came to Pauline. "I'll be back," she said. She walked down the stairs, over to the liquor cabinet, grabbed three glasses, and filled it with ice and rye whiskey. She glanced over and noticed Kenneth was busy helping with the removal of Anneliese's body. He saw her. She raised a glass, indicating she'd continue to keep Betty occupied for a while.

Pauline walked back upstairs into the bedroom, handing a glass to both women. They each took a sip of the fiery liquid. Setting her glass on the bureau, Pauline proceeded over to the wardrobe where Anneliese's dresses hung. She selected a brilliant red dress and held it up against her body.

"I remember her wearing this one," she said.

That was all it took. Betty grabbed another outfit and regaled the times she remembered when her mother wore it. Pauline and Betty continued doing this for the next hour. It was their way of letting the memories flow. Pauline told stories about the days when they were young. A few stories surprised Betty. They were new to her. It made her realize even more what a strong, independent, free-spirited woman her mother was. It brought a smile to her face. Despite the hard times she endured, it was heartwarming knowing she experienced good times as well.

After they finished, Betty selected the dress her mother would wear for the last time.

"Don't forget her dancing shoes," Pauline said. "She loved to dance. I know that's what she is doing now, dancing pain free."

The three women lifted their glasses.

"To Anneliese. Until we meet again."

The sound of ice clinking in their glasses could be heard as they raised them to their lips. Anneliese would definitely approve, preferring no tears and crying. She would have wanted to be toasted, just as they had done.

Betty was in excellent hands, surrounded by love and friendship.

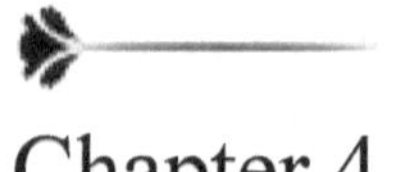

Chapter 4

etty woke to a warm spring day. It was unusual for Wisconsin to be so balmy this time of year. It was unlikely to last because it never did. Spring in the Midwest was unpredictable. The farmers were taking advantage of the temperature, plowing their fields and getting them ready for planting. The sun was glowing outside. It was unfortunate the weather did not match Betty's frame of mind.

She got out of bed, put on her housecoat, and sauntered to the kitchen. She made a pot of coffee. She needed as much help as she could today. Before finishing her second cup, the doorbell rang. Betty knew it was her friend before she even answered the door. Evelyn had insisted on staying with her ever since her mother passed. But after a couple of days, Betty sent her on her way. She wanted the time to be alone with her thoughts; especially on the eve of her mother's funeral. It had been a sleepless night. The memories keeping her awake.

When she opened the door, Evelyn stood in the doorway dressed in black, ready for the funeral. Betty hugged her friend in greeting with a heavy heart, grateful she was there. Back in the kitchen, she retrieved another cup and saucer out of the cupboard. She poured the strong, black liquid and handed the cup to her friend. Betty lit a cigarette before taking another sip.

"How did you sleep?" asked Evelyn.

"Not well."

"I understand it's hard. You will get through this."

"Sure, I will. It's just that I miss her so much."

"She will always be with you. She will forever be in your heart. It will get easier with time."

"I hope you're right because it hurts like hell right now."

"I'll help you get ready. Kenneth will be here any time. Let's go."

Betty crushed her cigarette butt into the ashtray. Evelyn grabbed her friend's hand and led her up the stairs to her bedroom.

"Sit. I will style your hair."

Evelyn started brushing out Betty's hair, smoothing it. Anneliese had always kept up on the popular clothes and hairstyles. Her daughter was no different. Evelyn began pulling the top half of her hair back behind her ears, making it as sleek as possible. She secured it with a medium-sized black bow, and then brushed the rest of Betty's shoulder length hair until it formed soft curls around her face.

Next, Evelyn started applying make-up. Her goal was getting rid of the dark circles under Betty's eyes from lack of sleep. She continued working her magic, applying the finishing powder last. Satisfied with her work, she turned Betty towards the mirror and said, "Betty, you're as gorgeous as your mother. You are your mother's daughter."

Tears threatened to prick Betty's eyes when Evelyn spoke those words, but she held back. She must handle herself in the manner her mother had whenever confronted by adversity. She needed to keep herself together.

Betty stood to hug her friend. "Call me Betz, like Kenneth does. It's time to start anew."

Evelyn smiled. "Not a problem, Betz."

It didn't take long before everyone was calling her Betz.

Betz slipped on a shirtwaist dress with a white collar. The short-sleeves were embellished with white cuffs. The style was one Ginger Rogers made popular from the film she did in 1940. They called it the Kitty Foyle. Betz was the proud owner of two. One in navy blue and one in black. The color black was the obvious choice for today. She slipped both feet into a pair of black baby doll shoes before turning to Evelyn.

"Well, here we go," she said as she took a deep breath.

The two women descended the stairs just as Kenneth reached the front porch, grabbing their handbags on their way out. Betz opened hers, making sure a handkerchief was easily accessible. Kenneth stopped Betz and kissed her on both cheeks. He opened the car doors for both women, waiting for them to slide inside before slamming it shut. It warmed Evelyn's heart, knowing her friend found a man as gentle and kind as Kenneth. She could see the love in his eyes whenever he looked at Betz. She hoped to be as lucky to find someone to appreciate her the same way.

Kenneth took his time driving to the funeral home, giving Betz the needed time to prepare herself for what was coming. He pulled up behind the hearse already parked in front. He got out, walked around the car, opening the door for his fiancé and her friend. They climbed the few stairs to the Ferguson Funeral Home, where her mother lay for the viewing. Mr. Ferguson greeted Betz as she crossed the threshold.

"Betty, I am so sorry. Your mother was a wonderful woman," he said.

She muttered thank you.

Turning to Kenneth, Mr. Ferguson shook his hand. He explained to them both where he wanted them to stand.

Kenneth led Betz to the front of the room. The sight of her mother lying in the casket, eyes closed, became more than she could bear. If it wasn't for Kenneth holding her elbow with a firm grip, she likely would have crumpled to the floor. With Kenneth by her side, she kneeled on the riser. Her private thoughts a jumbled mess.

Please, mother, give me the strength that you have always shown me. Help me get through today. I miss you so much. I'm not sure what I'm going to do without you. Please show me a sign you are ok.

She barely finished her thoughts when a loud bang resounded throughout the room.

"What was that?" Evelyn exclaimed in an excited voice. "It scared the living daylights out of me."

No one identified the cause of the loud noise. Nothing had broken or fallen that anyone could see. Betz remembered thinking how strange the timing was to her thoughts.

Kenneth helped Betz back to her feet to stand in the designated spot. Many people were arriving to pay their respects. A line was forming. Kenneth's parents were one of the first to present themselves. They had not known Anneliese well, having only met once after Kenneth proposed to Betz. They were there to support their son and future daughter-in-law.

Betz couldn't count how many times she heard the words "I'm sorry." The number of people flowing through the line to say goodbye to her mother overwhelmed her. People from Ruby's café, Becker Insurance, and the hospital came. All the places her mother had worked. The turnout was no surprise, Anneliese had lived in Brimmer her entire life.

The funeral was held at St. Francis Catholic Church the following day, including a full mass with communion. Betz struggled to pay attention to the sermon. She didn't think it'd ever end. Her mind not concentrating on the words spoken about God and heaven. Instead, she reflected on the life she shared with her mother.

Kenneth nudged her. They stood. The service was over. She placed her hand in the crook of his arm, slowly following the casket out of the church where the hearse waited. They drove to the cemetery with a caravan of cars following.

On a beautiful spring day, they laid her mother to rest alongside Anneliese's baby twin sister who died at birth. The sister her mother had not known existed until after Martha's death. It was bittersweet to see her mother's name engraved in the tombstone beside her only sibling. It was strangely comforting to think they may be together again.

Betz looked at her surroundings, wanting to remember this day, forever. Half dazed, she thought she saw someone looking at her from a distance. She turned away when Kenneth said something to her. When she looked again; the person was no longer there. It was probably just her imagination.

"Betz, it's time to go." Kenneth grabbed her elbow, leading her away.

She couldn't resist glancing back over her shoulder one more time at the coffin. It was hard saying goodbye. Her mother had been everything to her. Life without her will be different.

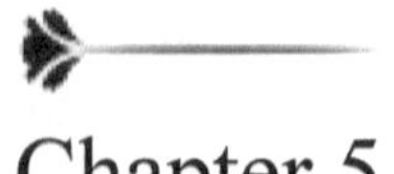

Chapter 5

The next few days passed in a blur. Betz was numb, moving through the motions. It was an odd sensation, being present without knowing what was actually happening. It felt as if her mind and spirit was disconnected from her body.

She had yet to return to work. Her boss, Mr. Becker, was an understanding man, allowing her the time she needed. He knew her mother well, being employed by him years ago, before Betz was born. Her mother took the position at Becker Insurance after returning home from the woman's college she attended. The one her parents sent her to after a fallout. They thought it would calm her spirit. From what Betz understood, it didn't.

Today, she had to get herself together. She was meeting the attorney to discuss the will. Kenneth was planning on meeting her there.

She dressed more carefully than she had over the past week. Betz glanced at her reflection in the mirror, trying to convince herself she could do this. She could sit and listen while her mother's wishes were read. It had to be done. She could not procrastinate any longer.

Betz got into the automobile and started up the engine. She jumped. The radio was blasting the song, 'Sentimental Journey.' It startled her. Immediately, tears welled up in her eyes pooling over onto her cheeks. She had a vivid memory of seeing her mother humming to this song, looking wistful. Betz had tiptoed away without interrupting, leaving her mother to her quiet thoughts. She turned the volume to a manageable level. It was as if Mother was telling her she was right there, riding in the seat beside her.

Oh, Mother, why did you have to die this soon?

It was challenging to sit and wait in the attorney's lobby. She glanced at her watch. It was unlike Kenneth to be late. The bell rang above the doorframe, and she saw Kenneth walking towards her, out of breath.

"Sorry to keep you waiting," he said.

"I wasn't sure you'd make it on time."

"I'll explain later."

There was no time to ask questions. Mr. McNamara's secretary instructed them to follow her, leading them into a large conference room. One wall composed of floor to ceiling windows with the view overlooking Brimmer's Main Street. Betz could see her office from here. Her mind drifted. She desired to get back to her job. There was work waiting for her and she missed her coworkers. *Soon,* she thought.

They sat at a round table placed in the middle of the room. Betz, nervously folded her hands in her lap, waiting. Mr. McNamara dominated the room when he walked in. He was a large man. He had a full head of hair that was graying. His suit was too large for him, making him look even bigger than he was. As he sat, the chair groaned with his weight. He greeted them, telling Betz how sorry he was for her loss. He shuffled the papers around before he began.

"The house, all its possessions and money are bequeathed to you," he said.

It was not a surprise. She was Anneliese's only daughter.

"Betty Doyle, your mother has left you nothing to worry about. She did the right thing. She left everything in order, making it as easy as possible for you." He said in an excited voice. He continued with the details. Kenneth squeezed her hand tight. He knew it was more than she could absorb.

Mr. McNamara looked at the paper in front of him. He revealed the amount of money she inherited.

She found her voice and asked. "How much money did she leave me?"

Mr. McNamara repeated the number. Betz gasped in disbelief. She tried to listen, but her mind kept straying. It was difficult to concentrate on his words.

"In summary, besides the house, your mother has left you a generous amount of funds." Mr. McNamara informed her.

Still in disbelief, she had another question to ask. "Did she leave anything else? Any other documentation she may have given you? Something of my birth? My father?"

"Sorry. I have nothing more," he said.

Betz sat in silence. Her feet rooted to the floor. He continued explaining about bank accounts and other miscellaneous items. Her brain remained elsewhere.

Finally, the meeting ended. She remembered shaking his hand before walking out of the office, towards her car. She was certain her mother left something with the attorney. Some information about her birth father. Her head in the clouds, she heard

Kenneth saying he'd see her tonight after work. With a shake of her head in agreement, she kissed him goodbye on the cheek. Totally distracted, she got into her car and fumbled in her handbag to find the keys. She didn't understand what just happened. Her mother had given her financial freedom but was unwilling to give her what she wanted the most: information regarding her father.

She started the car and drove towards the cemetery without realizing where she was going. She parked and began walking to her mom's gravesite. Her emotions were a jumbled mess. She felt sad, angry, and upset at the same time.

What was her mother's reason for being so elusive whenever she asked questions about her father?

She needed to talk to her. Ask her questions, even though she'd receive no answers from the grave.

In a daze, she walked to where she buried her mother more than a week ago. As she got closer, she noticed something lying on top of the tombstone. It was a lovely, single yellow rose. She surveyed the cemetery, looking for other clues. There was nothing more. She thought it strange. *Who would have done this?* Confident if it was someone she knew, they would have mentioned it to her.

Mother, did you have a secret admirer and not tell me?

Chapter 6

Kenneth arrived for dinner that evening. Betz, not known as the greatest cook, could still produce a decent meal. Tonight's menu included meatloaf, mashed potatoes, and green beans. They sat at the kitchen table tonight; it being cozier than the dining room. Betz was sullen as she dished food onto two plates. The dishes they were using were her grandmother's, the same ones they used every day growing up. Her mother made some changes in the home after her grandmother died, but getting rid of the dishware was not one of them. Maybe it was time Betz did. It conjured up too many memories.

Once they finished eating, Kenneth dried the dishes as Betz washed. Helping with dishes was atypical for a man, it being considered a woman's chore. But Kenneth simply didn't feel right, just sitting there watching her wash dishes without helping. After the last pot was dried, Betz filled the meatloaf pan with warm, soapy water to let it soak. She would clean it in the morning.

Kenneth seldom showed up on a weeknight, but he planned to have a serious talk with Betz regarding their plans for the future. Betz refilled both coffee cups before heading to the living room. Handing

Kenneth his, she relaxed on the lounger and lit a cigarette. Kenneth did the same.

Kenneth stroked her arm before speaking. "Betz, I want to become married as quickly as possible. I can't stand the thought of you living in this enormous house by yourself. I love you. We were planning on marrying this summer, anyhow. Let's do it sooner."

He sensed her hesitation. He wondered if it had something to do with the meeting today. "Betz, you know I will love and care for you always. I want us to begin a family. I can't wait to have children. This doesn't concern your inheritance. This has to do with us."

Speechless, she motioned for him to kiss her. He cocked his head, looking at her. What he saw, gave him no hesitation. He leaned towards her. The kiss conveyed everything they felt for each other: love, empathy, compassion, and longing. Once the kiss ended, Betz looked at Kenneth with love in her eyes.

"I know you love me. I have no doubt you will take care of me. I want nothing more than to marry you. It makes sense to get married as soon as we can. There is one thing holding me back. I assure you it has nothing to do with you."

"What is it?"

"You will think I'm being silly. I hate to even say this out loud to you."

"Come on, Betz. You know me better than that."

She took a deep breath. "Before we marry, I want to find my father. I haven't anyone to walk me down the aisle. No father, no mother, no uncles, no brothers. I have no one. I was so hoping Mother left Mr. McNamara with information about who my father is. I am disappointed. I swore to myself I'd search for him. At a minimum, I need to try. Please understand."

Kenneth leaned over and held Betz close. "Of course, dear. I'd never deny you something you consider important. Please promise me this. We will get married this fall. I don't want to wait any longer than that. That should give you enough time."

"I promise. We will marry before the trees lose their leaves."

They sat and talked for a while longer before Kenneth got up to leave. He had to be at the Bailey Oil Company early in the morning. He had been granted a transfer to Brimmer when he planned to propose to Betz. He understood his future wife would want to live close to her mother after they married. That was before Anneliese became ill. His transfer was granted, allowing him to be near Betz and her mother during the last months of her life. It made it easier for everyone.

Bailey Oil Company was a great company. They always supported him. When he was first hired, he landed a job in the warehouse, stacking barrels and keeping track of the freight inventory. When he transferred to Brimmer, he worked at the bulk plant. Kenneth earned a fair salary for the job he did. The semi drivers were independent contractors, earning better money. Kenneth hoped he could have his own truck with his own route someday. A goal to work towards.

Betz slept well that night. She woke the next morning with renewed energy, determined to find her father. A phone call to Mr. Becker, her boss, was first on the agenda. After hanging up the phone, she smiled. He was a fantastic boss. She wondered how she got so lucky. The people she worked with were great. She asked him for one more week to get everything in order. She remained hopeful it was enough time to find what she was looking for.

Before falling asleep the previous night, she put a plan together. The first thing she'd do was go through the house from top to bottom. There must be something here, giving her information about her father. She donned a cotton shirtwaist dress that buttoned in the front. It nipped her at the waist and had a flowing skirt. It was comfortable. A suitable outfit for the rigorous lifting she'd be doing today while looking for clues.

She started with her mother's bedroom. It made sense to Betz that her mother would keep her most private and precious possessions there. When she walked into the upstairs bedroom, for once, it did not upset her. She had an agenda, and was there to accomplish something. It was not a time to let emotions overcome her.

She started looking through the wardrobe. She stood on a chair in order to reach the top shelf. Being meticulous, she carefully lifted each box from where they rested. She placed them on the bed. Once she had everything off the closet shelf, she began her hunt.

The first few boxes had nothing in them except hats. Lovely though they were, it was disappointing. Another box contained doilies. She was sure they were ones her grandmother must have made. She laughed when opening up a small shoebox stuffed with dollar bills. When she counted, the amount added to fifty dollars. *How absurd!*

The next box contained cards and letters. As she rummaged through them, it was obvious they were from Anneliese's fiancé, Frank. He had died from the Spanish flu after returning home from WWI. Her mother told her stories about Frank. He was her high school sweetheart, and they planned on getting married as soon as he came back from the war. He had been her mother's first love. She had nothing but positive things to say about him. Looking at the letters, it was obvious how dear to her mother's heart Frank was.

Another box contained little trinkets of no significance. They looked like gifts for a child. It was something her mother most likely forgot she had. Since she lived in this house her whole life, there wasn't any reason to clean out closets. This one was tucked away in the corner, most likely forgotten.

Betz lifted the lid off the last box with a flutter of anticipation. Inside laid a book amongst other mementos. *Could this be it?* She could only hope.

Her fingers trembling, she removed the book from the box. Dismay came over her as she looked at the cover. Etched into the leather was the name St. Catherine's. It was memorabilia of her mother's time spent in the women's college. The school her parents sent her to after spending a night in jail after getting swept up in a police raid of a speakeasy. Betz flipped the pages, reading a few messages. They described escapades the women had together. Some appeared to be funny poems written about her mother's personality. It would be an interesting read. Someday, but not today, though. It wouldn't give her the clues she was searching for. The era didn't match. *Another day,* she told herself as she closed the book. Other items in the box were mementos of her time at school. Napkins, paper clippings, programs, a dried flower and a dance card were just a few.

Betz walked back to the closet, searching the floor. Nothing appeared out of the ordinary. She then made her way through every dresser drawer. Nothing. She looked under the bed. Nothing. She searched every nook and cranny in the bedroom. Nothing. With regained composure, she told herself she had only begun her search. This was only one room, and there were many more.

Disappointed, yet not willing to give up, she headed downstairs to the room they called the library. It was not your typical library seen in pictures. This one did not have floor to ceiling shelves holding hundreds of books. This room was much smaller. A large bookshelf her grandfather had built stood against one wall. Books of many genres collected over the years stood on the wooden shelves. A love for books is something she shared with her mother. They often got lost in stories. It was a distraction to focus on someone else when their own world appeared crazy, even though the characters weren't real.

Against the opposite wall sat a desk and chair. Her mother told her once that her grandfather used this room often. Her mother often found him sitting here in the early evening hours after work. She never understood what he did there, since he was not a businessman, and paperwork was not required for his job. It may have been his place to escape. Betz envisioned her own mother sitting at the desk to pay bills.

Hmmm. The desk is too obvious. There can't be anything in there.

Betz walked across the room with eagerness, seeing the papers and mail strewn on top of the desk. *I need to go through this stuff;* she reminded herself. She knew there was nothing of significance amongst those items since she had placed them there herself. Sitting on the chair, she opened the side drawers first. Nothing unusual there. Only the typical things one might expect to see in a desk drawer.

The last drawer she tried was the one in the middle. It was stuck when she tried to open it. She yanked on it, giving it a gentle yet firm tug. There, lying in the drawer, was a sealed envelope with her name written on it. Right away, she could tell it was her mother's handwriting. She held her breath.

Could this be it? Would this give her the answers she was seeking? At last, would her mother tell her the identity of her birth father?

With the envelope in hand, the gravity of the situation overcame her. No one understood what it meant to her to find the truth about her father. She grabbed the letter opener sitting amongst the other office supplies in the drawer. With caution, she slid the sharp edge along the top of the envelope. Tearing something important inside would be devastating. She stifled a sob when she recognized her mother's favorite stationery.

She began reading,

My Darling Daughter,

If you are reading this, then it means I am no longer with you. Thinking about that makes me very sad. You already know this, but I need to say it. I love you with all my heart. You were the best thing that happened to me. I wish I did not have to leave you so soon. Such is life. If there is life after death, I promise I will watch over you. I will be with you during your special moments in life.

It makes me thrilled you will not have any financial worries. Use the money I am giving you wisely. Your grandmother left us in a good financial position. She inherited money from her uncle. Be careful what you throw away. After the Great Depression, we removed money from the bank. There is money concealed throughout the house. I have left a separate list telling you where we hid money. Please be mindful, though. I may have forgotten places your grandmother, and I hid it.

It makes me ecstatic you have found Kenneth. He is a good man. Marry him. Don't wait. Start a family. This house needs to be filled with lots of children. Neither of us had that.

Don't cry for me. I had a wonderful life. You, most of all, brought me the greatest joy. I am thrilled you came into my life and we shared that life together.

Go, love that man of yours. Be happy.

Forever in my mind, evermore in my heart,

Your loving mother,

Anneliese

Unbeknownst to Betz, the tears began flowing down her cheeks immediately when she started reading. She swiped at them, unsure if they were ones of sadness or of disappointment. Her mother's words were beautiful, but the letter did not contain what she had hoped. She still had no inkling who her father was.

Chapter 7

Betz spent the week searching the house. She was looking for something, anything, leading her to her father's identity. She came up empty-handed. The attic contained interesting relics and antiques. Many she had never seen, or at least didn't remember. Her mother must have placed them there after her grandmother died. Some pieces looked even a generation older. She'd inspect them closer, at a later date, when she had more time.

Betz recalled how her mother changed the décor after her grandmother died. Her style reflected in the furnishings. She embarked on a shopping spree, buying modern pieces and placing them throughout the home. Betz remembered excitement when she'd come home from school, and Mother waiting to show her the new find of the day. Sometimes, the two of them shopped together. Those were great times.

Despite the new items her mother bought, she also kept items from the past. Betz was sure the older pieces meant something or triggered a memory for her mother. Things she couldn't part with.

Betz had no desire to change the furnishings. Maybe someday, but now was not the time. Her mother's presence still lingered wherever she looked. She preferred it that way.

Betz walked over to a trunk she hadn't noticed before. It was tucked in the corner with a small coverlet lying over it. She drew the cloth off, noticing the lock was not latched. A quick pull was all it took to release it. As she lifted the lid, she held her breath. Her stomach did a flip-flop. Her gut was telling her something of importance was held within.

Her eyes were immediately drawn to the identical baptismal outfits lying side by side. Her mother told the story of how she found them after her grandmother died. Her mother was saddened to discover her twin sister died a few days after birth. With a delicate hand, she lifted them up to discover a small box underneath. The contents within were random; New Year's Eve party favors, a pearl necklace, a pair of evening gloves, and a pressed flower. Betz gasped. The flower appeared to be a rose. *Could it be? Was this once a single yellow rose? What was its significance? What was the link to these things?* She placed the box on the floor. She'd take it downstairs and examine it more closely later.

Next, she pulled out two gorgeous gowns, wondering what importance they had. Beneath those, she saw a package, carefully wrapped. When she gingerly undid the ties, holding the wrapping in place, it revealed a white wedding dress. A rush of emotion came over her. She instinctively knew it was her mother's dress. Her mother never married, so she never got the chance to wear a wedding dress. Betz wondered if this was the dress she planned to wear when marrying Frank or perhaps she planned to wear it on her wedding day with Betz's birth father. A girl could dream, couldn't she?

There was no doubt in her mind that she'd honor her mother by wearing this dress at her own wedding. She wrapped it back up before leaving the attic. There was nowhere else to look. She had done a thorough search of the house without success.

The next step required a trip to the county courthouse. With any luck, documentation may lie within their walls, revealing her father's name. There had to be something there.

Anxious, Betz drove over to the town of Prescott. She climbed the stairs to the grand stone building. Under different circumstances, Betz would have taken in the architectural design, for the building she entered was quite impressive. Prescott was the county seat where the county legislature, county courthouse, sheriff's department headquarters, hall of records, jail and correctional facility were located. If any legal documentation existed, it would be here.

Betz followed the signs to the records department. Mrs. Fletcher sat at the front desk. It reminded Betz of the librarian in the local library. She asked for a copy of her original birth certificate. Mrs. Fletcher couldn't have been more helpful in locating it, making a duplicate copy and handing it to her. Immediately, Betz noticed the only parent listed on the document was her mother's name. The line was left blank under the heading of Father.

Mrs. Fletcher saw the disappointment in Betz's eyes. She had reviewed the document before making a copy, and noticed the lack of a father's name. It was not the first time someone sought information about their heritage. Now, knowing what she was looking for, Mrs. Fletcher referred Betz to other documents available. After several hours looking at newspaper articles, military records and other local records, Betz realized what she was looking for was impossible to find. She thanked Mrs. Fletcher for all the help she had given her, and left with a heavy heart.

Discouraged, but still hopeful, Betz drove back to Brimmer. There had to be someone in town who knows the facts about her birth. She drew a heavy sigh. It was unlikely anyone knowing the truth would tell her. If so, they'd already done so. However, that would not stop her from trying.

Betz loved and appreciated her mother's best friend, Pauline. She had been with her mother through all the hard times. She was sure she knew who her father was. Certain Pauline wouldn't divulge anything, she drove to her house, anyway.

Pauline, happy to see her friend's daughter, invited her in and offered her a drink. As each lit a cigarette, they toasted once more to Anneliese. They made small talk, chatting about the weather, the gossip in town, and how Betz was doing. Pauline asked about her plans for the wedding.

Betz saw an opening. She shared with Pauline her reason for the visit. Confessing, she felt desperate to find her father, hoping he'd want to share the joyous day with her. She described all the things she'd already searched, and how she hit a brick wall each time. Thus, the reason she was here. With pleading eyes, she asked her mother's friend if she could please reveal who her father might be.

Pauline shifted in her chair, unable to look at her. With scarcely a whisper, she told Betz.

"I can't tell you. I made a vow to your mother before you were born. I swore to never tell a soul the background or circumstances of your birth."

The disappointment on Betz's face made her sad.

"I begged her to share the story with you before she became too ill. Your mother told me it wasn't necessary. You were fine not knowing. There was no point telling you now. She reminded me of my promise to her. I was never to talk about it with anyone." Pauline hung her head.

"Betz, I'm so sorry. I can't live with myself if I broke the promise I made to your mother," Pauline apologized.

Incredulous, Betz bit her lip. She wished to argue. She wanted to scream. *Why? Why not tell me?*

Betz sensed nothing she said would change Pauline's mind. Who could blame her? Wouldn't she do the same for her friend Evelyn? She would never break her promise to her, either. It was her mother she was mad at, not Pauline. With reluctance, she told Pauline she understood.

Pauline grappled with having done the right thing. Saddened by Betz's reaction, she acknowledged she was the reason for it. She had the knowledge. She could have given her what she was seeking. Yet, a promise is a promise. One she was not willing to break, even though it was breaking her heart.

Chapter 8

Betz woke up on Monday morning, not sure how she was feeling. Today, she was returning to work after being gone for several weeks. Excited to see her coworkers but frustrated that she had not accomplished what she set out to do during her absence. Her emotions remained mixed. She would have limited time to look for her father now, and unsure where to look next.

As she drove the short distance to the office, an idea suddenly came to her. Hope ignited her spirits as she parked the car in the lot next to the building. She was positive Mr. Becker may know who her birth father was. Her mother worked for him until she gave birth. The father of her child certainly had to be discussed. The first opportunity she had she would ask him. She was confident he'd tell her if he did indeed have the knowledge.

She walked into the office, eager to talk to her boss. To her surprise, no one was at their desks. Instead, they were gathered in the break room. Betz could immediately tell something was wrong. Charlotte had her face covered with her hands and was sobbing. She overheard someone saying they couldn't believe it. Bill was trying to make a pot of coffee with little success. *What is happening?* She thought to herself.

Allen walked over and gave her a hug. "Glad to see you again, Betz. Welcome back. I wish circumstances were different."

She stared at him with questions in her eyes.

He explained. "Mr. Becker had a severe stroke. The doctors are unsure if he'll live. He may not make it through the week."

Betz grappled with the words Allen uttered. She felt sick to her stomach. It couldn't be. She had few men in her life, particularly someone as kind and generous as Mr. Becker. He was like a grandfather to her. Everyone would miss him, especially her. Thoughts were circling around in her head. One thought she could not shake, no matter how she tried. Mr. Becker and Andrew were the only ones who worked with her mother until she was born. Andrew moved out East a few years ago. Betz did not know where he lived. And now Mr. Becker was dying. She would never get the chance to ask him the questions she planned to. Her hopes, though brief, dashed once again.

Allen came to work at Becker Insurance after Andrew left. Today, he took charge. He announced for everyone to go home. There was nothing of importance needing done that couldn't be postponed for another day. Everyone gathered their things and left one by one.

Betz did not want to leave. Today was her first day back to work. She wanted to keep her mind occupied, so she stayed. She kept herself busy the entire morning, getting her desk and folders organized for the next day. When there was nothing more to do, she locked the office behind her after turning off the lights. She tugged the door, ensuring she locked it tight, engulfed with thoughts of Mr. Becker and his family. When the news of his death reached her later that day, she was not surprised.

Many people attended the funeral for Mr. Becker. He had lived in the community his entire life. His knowledge of insurance and graciousness as a man, is the reason Becker Insurance became the successful business it is today.

Betz's heart grew heavy when she saw Mrs. Becker standing by the oak coffin with a handkerchief pressed to her lips. She recognized the sadness in her eyes. It was the same sadness she saw in her own reflection. Death is a hard thing to accept. Everyone knows it will happen sometime, but when it happens to someone close, it turns your world upside down. She knew it better than anyone else.

Kenneth came up behind her and wrapped his arms around her waist. She was grateful he was there to support her. She turned to face him, seeing a stricken look in his eyes. *Oh, no, what else has happened?*

He touched her lips with his index finger. He whispered to her. "Later."

Betz sat through the service, wondering what news Kenneth had to share with her. She didn't think she was ready for whatever made his blue eyes look so troubled. Kenneth was trying his best to be there for Betz, but his mind was going a hundred miles an hour. Relieved when the funeral ended, the couple said goodbye, leaving with no one being the wiser, that something was amiss. Betz became anxious. Kenneth was a rock in these situations, but today, his hand trembled during the service, giving away something troubled him.

They had driven in separate cars, but Kenneth led her towards his vehicle. He opened the car door for her, motioning her to get inside. She looked at him with bewilderment in her eyes. He walked towards the driver's door with no words exchanged between them. She watched as he turned his head with a slight frown. He reached to the floorboard and retrieved a piece of paper, handing it to her.

Betz took it from him, her hands shaking. As she began reading, a queasy feeling developed in her stomach. Her eyes wide when she looked at him. He simply shrugged his shoulders. She continued reading. After she finished, she whispered. "This cannot be happening."

Kenneth was being drafted. He was to report to duty in a month.

Everyone thought war times were over after the surrender of the Japanese and Germans. The threat of communism was gaining momentum on an international level, the Cold War now extending to the borders of South and North Korea. With the support of Russia, North Korea launched an invasion into South Korean territory. It was all over the news. President Truman's administration feared continued communist invasions into other countries like the ones taking place in South Korea. It was time for the United States to step in. Communism had to be stopped.

Betz and Kenneth had kept themselves abreast of what was happening in Korea. They were concerned about the extent the US may enter the conflict. Once

President Truman committed troops to defend South Korea, and ordered a military draft requiring men between the ages of 18 to 35 serve their country. The two worried about the potential Kenneth would get called to serve. Kenneth, aware of deferments that may apply, foresaw nothing preventing him from being called. He now regretted he did not willfully sign up for the Marine Corps. Now that he received his draft letter, he did not have a choice to which branch he'd be assigned to. He'd be required to go wherever they wanted him. He did not relish that idea.

Betz let out a breath and swallowed, blinking away her tears. She spoke faster than she intended, "let's get married right away. I can't bear the thought of you leaving without us being married."

"What about finding your father first?" he asked.

"There's no time. You are more important to me. My father is no longer a priority. I have no clue where else to look, anyway. We can be married by a Justice of the Peace." she said.

Kenneth grabbed her, kissing her on top of her head. He held her, not wanting to let go. Scared of the unknown and his future, he chose not to let his apprehension show. He didn't want to lose her. War was unpredictable., but he swore to himself he'd return to her. He could not allow her to lose another person close to her.

The following week, Kenneth received a letter with his assignment details. He was being sent to the Marine Corps boot camp in Parris Island, South Carolina. He had to report at the end of the month for basic training. He received the news with trepidation.

It was official now. A little relieved, his assignment was not a different branch of the military. The Marine Corps was his first choice.

One evening, after Kenneth shared the news with her, Betz sat in her favorite chair recalling the letters she found in the attic. For all these years, her mother kept the correspondence her first love wrote to her during the war. She was unsure if her mother ever got over his death. Betz refused to let Kenneth leave without marrying him. Her mother never got the opportunity to marry her fiancé, and there was no way she'd risk letting that happen to her.

Chapter 9

Betz arrived at the courthouse, wearing a sheath dress overlaid with exquisite lace. It had a rounded collar with long sleeves. It accentuated her small waistline. A perfect fit for her petite figure. On her head she wore a shoulder length tulle veil. In her hands, she carried a bouquet of white gardenias and orchids.

Betz could hardly contain her excitement when she found the newspaper pattern used to bring this dress to life. The date on the newspaper validated her suspicion. Her grandmother, a well-known seamstress, took meticulous care to sew this gown for her mother's wedding to Frank. It was obvious from the thread work throughout. She was proud to be wearing a dress her grandmother had created. A dress never worn until today. Betz beamed. She was getting married today.

As she walked towards him, Kenneth thought to himself what a lucky man he was. No one looked lovelier than his bride did today. He turned to his brother, his best man, and smiled. His brother returned the gesture, understanding the importance of the day. When Betz smiled, it took Kenneth's breath away.

He brushed his lips on both her cheeks, whispering in her ear how much he loved her. He greeted Evelyn,

Betz's maid of honor, introducing her to his brother. The four stood together in the corridor, waiting for their names to be called. A couple exited the chambers with huge smiles on their faces. Apparently, they were not the only ones being married today.

"Doyle and Johnson," the clerk announced. The bride and groom with their witnesses walked to the front of the chambers. The judge shook hands, confirming who they were and instructing everyone where to stand. Wasting no time, the ceremony began. Before she knew it, Betz was saying, "I do." She heard the judge pronounce them husband and wife. Just like that, she had become Mrs. Kenneth Johnson. She felt exhilarated.

After leaving the courthouse, they traveled to Ruby's Café where a small crowd gathered to help them celebrate. The atmosphere filled with laughter and joy. Betz was thrilled with the compliments she received about her dress and how gorgeous she looked. People congratulated Kenneth on how lucky he was. The day was perfect.

As they drove home, Betz couldn't stop talking about how wonderful everything had been. Kenneth moved his things into the house earlier that week. He kept looking at her from the corner of his eye, sensing her nervousness. She was his wife now. He couldn't be happier.

They walked together to the house. The door opened easily when Kenneth inserted the key. Suddenly, he gathered Betz in his arms and carried his bride over the threshold. Once inside, still in his arms, he gave her a lingering kiss. She looked into his eyes and saw nothing but love.

The couple walked upstairs, taking their time before reaching the bedroom. They intended to savor these moments. They only had a week to spend together before Kenneth left. The discovery of each other took precedence. After making love, their closeness became even stronger. They laid in each other's arms, expressing what they meant to one another. After a while, Betz listened to Kenneth's deep breathing. He had fallen off to sleep. She loved this person with all her heart. She couldn't imagine life without him.

The newlyweds spent the next week preparing themselves for Kenneth's departure. He made sure everything in the house was in working order. He did not want his wife dealing with household problems while he was gone. He wanted to help her all he could before he left.

In the evenings, they sat on the front porch talking, watching the sunset, sharing their dreams. They needed this time together. Every moment counted. They spent the night caressing each other, sharing intimate moments as husbands and wives do.

The bus taking him to the train station was leaving on Saturday at ten o'clock. Kenneth's bags had already been packed. Not surprisingly, he was not the only man leaving Brimmer to report to duty. Families came to say goodbye to their loved ones. It was heartbreaking to see small children clinging to their father's legs, not wanting them to leave. Fathers were not exempt from the war.

The Johnsons were struggling with their own emotions. They were grateful for the time they spent together this past week. Betz thought she was better prepared for this moment. The two suddenly found it difficult to express themselves. They gave up, husband and wife standing there, embracing each other, not saying anything. They understood how much they meant to each other.

The bus driver yelled, "last call."

Kenneth was unwilling to let go.

Betz wiped at her eyes, telling herself not to cry. It was she who pulled herself apart from his loving arms. He gave her one last kiss before stepping onto the bus.

Kenneth took a seat by the window. He pressed his palm against the glass. He mouthed, "I will return to you. I love you."

She gulped, forcing herself to move. Without realizing what she was doing, she ran alongside the bus until she no longer could.

"You better come back to me," she shouted, making sure he heard her.

Gasping for breath, she saw the bus turning the corner in the distance and heading towards the highway. She brushed at the tears threatening to cascade down her face, her breathing returning to normal again. Aimlessly, she started walking down Main Street with no destination in mind. As she passed by the local recruiting office, something caught her eye. A poster with a military nurse made her stop. A memory of her mother telling her how she helped at the hospital during the pandemic came to her. *Could she do the same thing? Learn a new trade? Do something different with her life?* The idea of becoming a nurse created a sensation in her belly, a zealousness she seldom felt. It'd give her something to concentrate on during Kenneth's absence.

Excitement took hold. She could not stop thinking about her plans the entire weekend. After work on Monday, Betz drove to the community hospital to inquire about their nursing programs. She was introduced to the head of nursing, Mrs. Schwingl. To Betz's delight, the lead nurse informed her they were looking for women interested in a nursing assistant program here at this hospital.

"The war has made nurses scarce," she said. "Though a nursing degree is only being offered in the larger cities, nursing assistant programs are being provided in the local hospitals. We need the help."

Betz signed the papers that day. She knew this was something she wanted to do.

Curled up on the sofa that evening, she sat with pen and paper in hand. The letter to her husband telling him she was quitting her job and taking nursing classes may come as a surprise to him. She knew he'd be excited for her. She was doing something for herself. In the letter, she expressed how much she adored and missed him, and hoped to hear from him soon.

As she undressed, putting on her nightgown, it occurred to her how life had taken a different course in such a short time. Before drifting off to sleep, she thought, *Mother would be so proud.*

Chapter 10

The bus ride to the train depot passed swiftly. Kenneth's mind became occupied with thoughts of Betz and their future together. It was unfortunate he had to leave his wife so soon after just being married. They wished to start a family, but it would have to wait upon his return.

His thoughts shifted towards providing for his family. He believed becoming a trucker was the right choice for them. Once he returned home from the war, he planned to discuss with Betz about investing in his own semi to haul fuel. He could continue working for the Bailey Oil Company, but with a different job. The major fuel hub was close by. He was sure they could remain living in Brimmer. There would be no need to move. At least, he hoped so.

The bus came to a halting stop, forcing Kenneth out of his daydream. He waited for his bag to be unloaded. Grabbing it, he walked towards the train, that would take him to his next destination. Not understanding why, the number of men boarding the train surprised him. It shouldn't have. The state's major thoroughfare was this one. As he stood on the platform, he wondered how many men volunteered versus being drafted like him. When he looked around, he saw apprehension in their eyes, not unlike his own. None of them knew what to expect when they arrived at boot camp. Those who survived WWII told stories. It wasn't for the faint of heart. He knew they had a tough road ahead.

He once again took a window seat, wishing to view the landscape as he traveled to the East Coast. He had never ventured far from his home state before. Not that he didn't consider himself adventurous, but there was never a reason to travel. He would take advantage of this opportunity to see other parts of the country.

A tall, thin, muscular man similar in age with red hair and a ruddy complexion stopped in the aisle. He asked if the seat next to him was taken. Kenneth shook his head no. He threw his bag in the overhead compartment and sat in the empty seat.

"Hi, my name is Paul."

"Kenneth. Nice to meet you, Paul. Where are you headed?"

"Basic training. Parris Island, South Carolina."

"Me too. You drafted or volunteer?" Kenneth asked.

"Drafted. There was no time to volunteer. I got my letter before I had the chance to talk to the recruiting office. I'm just happy they assigned me to the Marines and not the Army."

"Ditto."

Kenneth discovered Paul was unmarried, but had a girlfriend. He worked as a welder in a plant in southern Wisconsin. He moved a lot, having lived in places throughout the Midwest, not staying in one place long.

Paul was a superb storyteller. Kenneth enjoyed hearing his adventures, laughing at many of them. A few escapades sounded dangerous. Kenneth thinking it impossible to live the way this guy did. Paul marveling at how anyone could be content with the life Kenneth chose. Regardless of their differences, they enjoyed each other's company throughout the journey to the coast.

The train pulled into the station, coming to a screeching stop. As they disembarked, they immediately got on another bus waiting to take them to their final destination, Parris Island, the place they called home for the next twelve weeks.

Once they arrived at boot camp, they were ushered off the bus. Wasting no time, they were taken into a reception hall, and given a questionnaire containing several pages to complete. Paul made a joke Kenneth did not hear. Other men around him chuckled. Paul was merely trying to lighten the seriousness of their whereabouts.

The drill sergeant marched in with authority and introduced himself. He made it clear what he expected from them.

"'Sir' better be the first word you utter. Always look straight ahead when addressed. I don't want to see anything different, no matter what," he barked.

Kenneth, now nervous, wondered how he was going to survive this.

Once the drill sergeant left, the men were handed a white cotton towel. They were told to place it around their necks with no other explanation. They were then led to another building. As they proceeded outside, they passed the Iwo Jima statue. The sight of it hit Kenneth hard. This was becoming very real.

Orders to strip from their civilian clothes were yelled out for all the men to hear. They were instructed to throw them into a waste barrel. Kenneth quickly realized what the towel's purpose was for. Men removed it from their neck and tied it around their waist. It was the only thing covering their private parts after their clothes were removed.

With only a towel wrapped around their waist, the guys waited their turn to have their heads shaved. Kenneth sat, hearing the clippers buzzing close to his ear. He felt the blade as it traveled up his neck, over the top, stopping when it reached his forehead. His hair dropped to the floor. He had always been proud of his thick, curly hair and now it just lay there amongst the others. There was something symbolic there. Something he didn't quite understand yet.

After they shaved his head, Kenneth headed towards the showers. He scrubbed his body from head to toe. A uniform, folded to perfection, was issued to him when he finished. He swiftly dressed, fumbling with the buttons on his shirt, evidence of his nervousness.

Shoe fit was important. Great care was taken in ensuring each man's shoes fit to perfection. It made it difficult to perform drills with traumatized feet, Kenneth overheard someone saying. Kenneth slipped his foot into the Brannock device. A size ten pair of combat boots was chosen for him.

After issuing their gear, they were told to return to the barracks. Each person was assigned a bunk. Kenneth was grateful he was far from the door, in the middle. He threw his bag on the mattress, thinking to himself he must be having a nightmare. No way this was happening.

After dinner, Kenneth sat on the edge of his bed, and wrote Betz a letter. Before he finished, the drill instructor came into the room. It was time for evening prayer. The men stood by their bunks, bowing their heads in a moment of silence. Each man given the chance to pray what they wished.

Please, give me strength to make it through this. Please, allow me to return to Brimmer, was all he could muster, relieved to have this day finally end.

Chapter 11

Betz woke up excited. Today was the day she'd begin learning to be a nurse. She quit her job at Becker Insurance the previous week. It had been difficult saying goodbye. She considered the people she worked with, friends. A lot had happened in her life recently. A change is exactly what she needed. They hated to see her go, but wished her well in her new endeavor.

She arrived early, a Doyle trait, leaving nothing to fate. It was the worst feeling in the world, being late. She hated that. To avoid it, she always allowed herself extra time. She'd rather be the one waiting, rather than being the person they waited for.

When she appeared at the nurses' station, she breathed a sigh of relief. She saw a woman from the American Red Cross and walked towards her, introducing herself. "Hello, I'm Betz Johnson." The word "Johnson" did not easily roll off her tongue, her married name still unfamiliar to her ears. Directed to wait in the lounge until the others arrived, she anxiously sat on the edge of a chair, legs crossed.

Betz took in her surroundings. It was always her desire to help others. She now had her chance. She intended learning as much as possible. One day, she may get the opportunity to become a full-fledged nurse. For now, she was satisfied to provide any help she could.

Soon, the other women arrived. Betz noticed two ladies her own age. After introductions were made, instructions were given. There was no time to waste.

The weeks after became a blur. She was quick to learn terminology the medical staff used. They showed her the proper manner to handle patients. It varied according to their condition. She was unaware of the enormous effort needed to care for patients until she did it herself.

She discovered many things about herself during this time. She had a knack with patients, getting them to do things they sometimes refused. She was a good listener, a good communicator. She enjoyed every facet of what she was doing, though tiring it was.

Betz became friendly with the other trainees. They'd often meet for lunch breaks when time allowed. Tina Campbell was quiet and serious. She came from a large family, and still lived at home. She was not one to share a lot, but had a bubbly laugh that was contagious.

Marj Nelson was the opposite. She was outgoing, friendly, and ambitious. She was easy to like. She lived in Lansbury, traveling to Brimmer each day. She married her high school sweetheart, who was also fighting in the war. Betz found they had a lot in common. They got along splendidly. Marj also wished to become a nurse. A goal certain she'd attain. They'd sometimes dined together after a long shift, both enjoying each other's company.

Betz wrote to Kenneth often, updating him on everything she was being trained to do. She told him how fulfilling and exciting it was to help people. How it gave her purpose. She loved and missed him horribly, but wanted him to know she was doing well. She received a few letters back from Kenneth. Not as many as she would like. He was managing, but she detected homesickness and loneliness in his words.

One day, they assigned Betz to a nurse caring for mothers in the delivery room. Two mothers arrived within minutes of each other, causing chaos. The two moved between patients, trying to meet their needs. Both mothers ready to give birth any time. It was an exhilarating day. Betz got to witness the birth of a boy. After that, a girl. It was a day to remember.

The next morning, she woke up not feeling well. She vomited in the bathroom. *I must have eaten something rotten yesterday;* she thought to herself. The queasiness in her stomach ceased when she began dressing for another day at the hospital. She hoped it was nothing contagious. She didn't give it another thought throughout her busy day.

The following morning, she woke up with more nauseousness in her midsection. As she trudged back to bed after using the bathroom, she straightened her back with a jolt. *It can't be!* But knew it was true. From the medical books she had been reading, and the stories she heard from mothers, she knew she was pregnant. The doctor confirmed it the following week.

She was ecstatic. She was going to be a mother. It is what she hoped to happen. She had been using the Wonder Pill ever since she planned to marry Kenneth. A pill the doctors recommended for those wanting to become pregnant. Millions of women were taking

DES as a prenatal vitamin. She learned in her short time at the hospital that it contained a synthetic estrogen that helped to prevent miscarriages. It made her sad thinking Kenneth was finding out he was a father in a letter. Yet, she couldn't wait to tell him the great news.

Betz did not tell anyone at the hospital she was pregnant. She worried it may jeopardize her position as a student. She wanted more time before she told them. She wished to absorb as much knowledge she could before leaving the program.

There was no stopping her from calling Evelyn to tell her the good news, though. Evelyn recently moved to Lansbury, finding work in a large company as a secretary. Unable to see each other as often as they liked, they talked on the phone frequently. Evelyn was surprised but happy for Betz. She reassured her she would be there if she needed anything.

The letter she received from Kenneth conveyed both excitement and worry. Delighted to become a father, he was anxious. He wasn't able to be there with her. He expressed his love and concern in a loving and kind way. She loved him with her whole being.

Betz tired more than usual over the course of the next few weeks. She was on her feet all day long, but enjoying what she was doing. She told herself she could sleep and relax over the weekend. One of the few advantages of living by herself.

She slept past 8 o'clock on Saturday morning. That was unusual for her. When she got up, she made herself some strong, black coffee. She still felt tired.

Tomorrow was her mother's birthday. She planned on visiting the gravesite.

As the day continued, thoughts of becoming a mother overwhelmed her. This was the start of her dream. She desired a large family and wanted nothing more than to fill the house with children.

Part of her weekend chores was to dust the furniture and vacuum the rugs. Though she promised herself to take it easy, she did not wish to neglect her self-imposed duties. Once they were completed, she laid on the bed to nap. When sleep eluded her, she wrote Kenneth a long and loving letter.

A sudden, sharp pain traveled through her abdomen. It forced her to double over, trying to reduce the pain. Another one came soon after the first one ended. She gasped until the pain subsided. Somehow, she found her way to the bathroom. When she sat on the toilet, she noticed blood on her undergarment. She was spotting. It didn't take medical experience to understand what was going on with her. She was having a miscarriage. She was losing her baby.

When she stood, she saw the blood mixed with the urine in the toilet. There was more blood than she expected. Knowing there could be complications, she called Evelyn. Sobbing, she told her friend what was transpiring. Evelyn promised she'd come right away.

Throughout the day, Evelyn held Betz's hand and kept a damp cloth on her forehead. The cramping and bleeding came to a halt near midnight. Once they were sure it was over, Evelyn drew a bath. When Betz slid into the water, her body went limp. Devastated beyond belief, she stayed there until she was covered in goosebumps. She forced herself to step out of the bathtub before she caught a cold. With a towel wrapped around her, she walked back into the bedroom, noticing Evelyn had changed the sheets. After putting on her nightclothes, she slid underneath the covers. She had no energy left. Evelyn brought a hot, cup of tea for both of them.

Evelyn crawled into bed next to her friend just as they did when they were young girls, holding her in her arms as she wept. She brushed her hair back with her hand, trying to soothe her the best she could. Evelyn refrained from telling her she was young. They could try again. Though the words were true, saying them would be of no comfort.

Amongst the tears, Betz told her friend she had been taking the Wonder drug to prevent what just happened. Evelyn listened, and became alarmed. She had just read an article about this pill. Several physicians thought DES did the opposite of what it was touted to do. They thought it was actually causing miscarriages instead of preventing them. It wasn't time to tell her friend what she feared.

After a fitful night of sleep, the two women woke early. They trudged to the kitchen half asleep. Coffee is what they both needed. Evelyn let Betz talk. Like most women when they lost a child, she wondered what she did wrong. She began to go over every detail, wondering what she had done to cause her to lose the baby. Evelyn reassured her it was nothing she did. She then told her what she had read. Betz was appalled.

"I would not have taken it if I knew it caused harm," she said in an alarming voice.

"You are not alone. They are just understanding what this drug is doing," Evelyn responded.

Betz threw the pills out that day. She will take her chances the natural way. She didn't want to relive that anguish ever again.

Later in the day, Betz convinced Evelyn to return home. Today was her mother's birthday. She had plans to visit her grave, needing to talk to her. She missed her so much. Evelyn made her promise to call if she needed anything. Betz promised, thanking her for coming to be with her. They hugged each other goodbye.

Betz drove to the cemetery in a gloomy mood. She walked among the headstones until arriving at her mother's site. She could not believe what she was seeing. She twirled around to look if there was anyone nearby. There was no one but her. She turned back, facing the grave. There, once again, lay a single yellow rose on the tombstone.

Collapsing to her knees, Betz traced the letters engraved in the granite. It was only a few months, yet it still hurt, especially today. She was still weak and tired from the previous night's catastrophe. The grass was warm when she sat, resting her back on the stone, sitting in the afternoon sun. Betz sat in silence until the anger took over.

"How could you leave me?" she wailed. "I lost a baby. Your grandchild. I needed you. I need you. I can't do this alone."

Unable to hold back any longer, her body wracked with sobs she had been holding back. There was no need to appear brave today. She could care less about being the strong woman she was portraying to be with everyone. Life presented a multitude of reasons for her not to be. She was tired, exhausted. She blamed herself for losing the baby even though deep down she knew it wasn't her fault. It was not meant to be, but she couldn't avoid feeling guilty.

I wonder if it was a boy or a girl?

Distracted by the yellow rose lying there, her sobbing stopped. Unknowingly, she picked it up, wondering who it was that left it there. *It had to be someone fond of Mother. Who could it be?* Pauline denied placing the one there after the funeral. It wasn't her.

Betz could tell by the sun's position it was getting late. It was time to return home. Rest is what she needed, and a good, strong brandy. She stood to leave, placing the rose where she found it. Eager for a cigarette, she reached in her pocket and drew one out, placing it between her lips before lighting it.

She kept things inside for too long. It was cathartic to speak aloud. In a regretful voice, she told her mother she was sorry for being angry. She'd do better. It was just that she loved and missed her every day.

As she strolled back to the car, Betz recognized a renewed perseverance within herself. It was later she remembered she forgot to wish her mother a happy birthday, her main reason for coming today.

Betz wrote Kenneth a heartbreaking letter that evening, telling him she lost the baby. She made light of what she physically went through, not wanting him to worry. She assured him she had not been alone. Evelyn stayed by her side, making sure she was fine. The mental anguish she put herself through was not something she shared either. She needed to handle it in her own way. She apologized to him, knowing how much he wanted a family. It was hard not sharing her complete thoughts with him, but she didn't want him to feel guilty for not being here. He had enough to worry about. He was dealing with his own stress.

Unable to get the yellow rose off her mind, she called the one florist in town. She told them her name and the reason for the call. Since Mrs. Kent, the owner, knew her, she was forthcoming about giving her what little information she had. An anonymous person paid for a single yellow rose to be placed at Anneliese Doyle's gravesite every year on her birthday for the next twenty years. They sent cash, so the person remained nameless.

As she finished the call, Betz, flabbergasted at what she just learned, thought to herself. *Who does that? And why be so secretive? Who are you?* It made no sense. *Mother, what secrets did you keep?*

She didn't have time to dwell any further. She had to get to the hospital for her shift. No longer needing to quit the program since she lost the baby, she became more determined than ever to learn whatever they'd teach her. She became an astute student, spending her spare time reading medical books available to her. The nursing staff often requested she be the person to go on rounds with them.

One nurse in particular, Mae Wilson, took her under her wing. Mae knew her mother from the days of the pandemic, when Anneliese became part of the women's brigade and drove an ambulance during the crisis. Mae worked for years as a nurse. She was full of knowledge. Impressed with Betz's quick study, and pleased with the work she was doing, mentoring her was a pleasure.

The medical field fulfilled Betz. Even if her role was assisting the nurses, she felt needed. When home, alone, it became another story. Nobody needed her there. The house was empty. She spent time in an upstairs bedroom, the one she planned to turn into the nursery. She wanted a family, but it was taken from her. Unable to let go of feeling responsible, depression overcame her. Not in the mood to cook, she started to lose weight. The nights were too quiet, with her thoughts too strong. It took effort to hide her depression during the daytime, but somehow, she managed.

Marj sensed something different in Betz. After a shift, she asked her to meet for dinner. They had become friends, and she intended to find out what was causing her distress. They planned on meeting at Ruby's café.

Marj, being direct, asked what was wrong before they were barely seated. Betz, hesitant to share, acted surprise by her question. Marj pressed. Betz looked up from her plate. The story of the miscarriage spilled forth. She admitted feeling responsible for losing her baby. Guilt consumed her. She swept away her tears, feeling foolish.

Marj grabbed her hand across the table and reprimanded her. "Stop it this minute. What happened is not your fault. You know that. There are a dozen reasons that cause miscarriages. We've learned that."

"Logically, I understand that, but my heart won't allow me to let it go," Betz said in return.

Marj continued to have rational answers about everything. A frank discussion was precisely what Betz needed. Before leaving, she hugged Marj, thanking her for making her feel better about herself. It was time she pulled herself out of her misery.

Kenneth was devastated when he received Betz's letter. He cried, thinking of her there without him by her side when she lost the baby. He sensed she had not told him everything. It was obvious she was making light of a bad situation. *This damn war.* He was counting the days until he returned home, boot camp ending soon. He'd have two weeks to spend with her before his next assignment. It could not come soon enough.

It was a momentous day when Kenneth graduated from boot camp, relieved to have a brief respite. He was going home to his beloved Betz. Unable to contain his excitement, he said goodbye to his buddies. They spent twelve weeks in South Carolina together. He was uncertain if he'd ever see any of them again, each one receiving separate orders, assigned to different commissions.

Kenneth was overjoyed to learn he would not be attending infantry training. Instead, he was being assigned to a special support team. A team, he was told, that provided the front lines with petroleum products. They'd support both the ground troops and aviation. He told himself he drew the lucky card.

It took several days traveling back to his hometown of Brimmer. When Kenneth stepped off the final bus at his destination, Betz stood, waiting to greet him. The embrace they shared brought tears to those watching. Taking a step apart, they looked at each other. They appeared the same, but yet different. The experiences they both had during their time apart forced them to grow up fast.

They spent the next two weeks getting to know one another again. They shared their private thoughts with each other. Kenneth, conveying his dread of going overseas. Betz expressing her guilt over the loss of the child. Finally, explaining to him she thought the pills she had taken caused it. She asked for forgiveness.

Kenneth took her in his arms, assuring her it was not her fault. He lifted her chin and kissed her. They tenderly made love, wanting to take their time. Afterwards, they laid there happy and content. Their thoughts only on each other. He raised her hand to his mouth, kissing her palm. When she looked into his eyes, she saw no blame, only love.

The time flew quickly. Betz once again said goodbye to her husband. His special training was scheduled to last only a few weeks. After that, he'd be sent directly overseas to the warzone. Military duty was not their choice, but they loved their country. They could survive this.

Chapter 12

The weeks spent at special training were not as grueling as boot camp. Once completed, Kenneth wrote Betz one more time before leaving for South Korea. After he got there, he was unsure if she'd receive his correspondence. Not knowing what to expect in a foreign country made him apprehensive. He did not want her thinking this letter may be the last one she may receive from him, so he kept it lighthearted, although his heart was breaking. It was one of the hardest things he'd done.

The flight over was uneventful. Once the team settled in, their work began. Being assigned to one of the fuel depots meant one day he'd transport fuel to fighter planes. The next day, he may be transporting fuel for motorized units on the front lines. He never knew where he'd be ordered to go. Every day was unpredictable.

The North Koreans understood how important fuel was for the US military, and they did their best to eliminate all threats. Kenneth's group became one of their targets for mortar and sniper attacks.

One day, Kenneth and his team were hauling fuel to the front lines when an explosion in front of them made them stop dead in their tracks. Unsure what to do next, they continued the route, driving around the fiery blaze. When they arrived close to their destination, the captain in charge instructed them where to go. The fuel was desperately needed. Additional soldiers were sent alongside them, ensuring the successful delivery. Fortunately, no one was severely injured.

That night, Kenneth wrote Betz, telling her how he hated the war. He didn't understand why they were there. His frustration was overwhelming. It was more difficult than he imagined.

Betz kept herself busy at the hospital, volunteering to stay late whenever the opportunity arose, a way to keep herself occupied. It kept her mind off how much she missed Kenneth.

She spent her weekends continuing to search for her father. She researched newspaper clippings, particularly the year she was born. She was hoping to find an announcement that happened in her area. Something that may explain his absence. She wasn't giving up on this endeavor, but constantly coming up empty-handed was exasperating.

Persistent, she searched the bookshelves in the office more. Amused when she found money hidden in random books. There was no rhyme or reason. She thought it bizarre, wondering where the idea came from to hide it here. The list her mother left her did not include the places she was discovering. No wonder her mother told her to be careful. It was never large sums, but the small amounts began to add up.

Desperate to do something different for a change, she invited herself to Evelyn's. A day spent in Lansbury may do her good. She arrived early Saturday morning. First, they shopped for clothes. Exhausted from trying on outfits, they stopped for lunch at Vern's Diner. It was across the street from the Walsh and Connolly lumber store. The diner was a popular place to eat. Seated at the window, the two women watched people enter and leave the store as they talked nonstop.

"Wow, I did not know how busy a lumber store could be. The owners must be thrilled," Betz said.

"It's well known in town. People come from all over. The owners who started the business are actually friends. One is married with four kids. The other never married. He's a rather attractive man with money and everyone wonders why." Evelyn laughed.

"Interesting," Betz said, taking a spoonful of her delicious dessert. Betz noticed two people coming out of the store. "There's a handsome couple," she said.

Evelyn looked out the window. "Oh, that's Mr. Connolly, one of the partners," Evelyn said. "I can't fully make him out from here, but I'm quite certain that's him."

Betz followed the couple with her eyes. She noticed they walked off in opposite directions. As she watched them disappear, she turned her attention back to the conversation and her dessert. She was having a lovely time with her friend.

After paying the bill, they drove to the grocery store, picking up ingredients needed for dinner. Once they arrived home, they placed the items in the refrigerator. They poured themselves a glass of wine before they meandered to the living room. They spent the rest of the afternoon, chatting.

Evelyn talked about her job. She enjoyed living in Lansbury. There was more to do there. Betz knew her friend had recently met a guy. To her delight, Evelyn was giddy over him, telling her how special he made her feel. Evelyn was looking forward to seeing where the relationship led. She couldn't wait for Betz to meet him.

Betz told Evelyn everything happening at the hospital, how much she loved the medical field and helping people. She was so inspired by what she was learning. It was one of the best decisions she made, something she was doing for herself.

Evelyn saw how excited Betz was with her new undertaking.

Still baffled by the yellow rose's significance left on her mother's gravesite, Betz confided how she romanticized it was her father who left it there. Evelyn knew her friend's desperation to know the story of her birth. She didn't blame her. It was a mystery indeed. She never discouraged her constant search. However, Evelyn feared she may face disappointment if she ever learned the truth. It may be a story to be left untold.

Discussion about the miscarriage was unavoidable. Betz expressed gratitude for Evelyn's help through the traumatic event. She felt fortunate she had not been alone. The subject of the Wonder Pill came up. Betz talked about the guilt she felt for taking it, even though it was recommended by doctors.

Evelyn said the words she'd been waiting to say.

"You can get pregnant again, Betz. Kenneth will be home before you know it."

For a moment, the world stood still. Betz met Evelyn's eyes with a meaningful expression. Betz jumped to her feet, grabbing her friend and hugging her.

"Oh, my goodness, Evelyn. It took you to say those words out loud to make me realize. I'm pregnant again. I didn't give it any thought. I haven't been sick, this time. I was secretly hoping I'd get pregnant when Kenneth was home on furlough, but wasn't keeping track of how many weeks it's been. It's too good to be true."

Evelyn's eyes flickered in surprise. "Are you sure?"

"I'm sure."

Evelyn grabbed Betz and swung her around in a circle, delighted with the news.

The doctor confirmed the pregnancy the following week. She wrote to Kenneth, hoping the letter would bring some joy. He was going to be a father. They already discussed names when talking about the family they wanted. If it was a girl, she'd be named after her mother, Anneliese. If it was a boy, they'd name him Will. She promised her husband she'd be extra careful. She wanted nothing to happen this time.

Paranoid of having another miscarriage, Betz read numerous books about pregnancy. So many, it made her head spin. Opinions differed amongst the professionals. *Who does one believe?* she wondered. She became overly cautious, afraid something she did would cause harm to the baby. One reference struck a chord with her. It stated the unborn can sense stress and anxiety from the mother. From that moment on, she stopped worrying and began enjoying her pregnancy.

Chapter 13

The weeks and months faded away. Betz looked at herself in the mirror, laughing. Her belly taking over the entire silhouette when she turned sideways. She wished Kenneth was there to share the joy. The pregnancy was going well. She felt good. She loved being pregnant. She wanted this experience again and again.

One of her favorite things to do was draw a bath with warm, sudsy water. When she slid into the tub, she placed her hands on her stomach, waiting for the baby to kick. This baby loved the warm cloth she placed on top of her round stomach. *Ugh!* The foot of her small infant kicking, pierced her ribs. Instead of grimacing in pain, she held her breath before smiling. The movement meant her baby was healthy. Nothing made her happier. She soaked her aching body as long as she was able. This baby will change her life forever, and she couldn't wait.

The doctor tried to give her a diet pill when she gained more weight than expected. She refused. She was not willing to risk taking any medication while pregnant. Betz was taken aback when he suggested she watch what she ate. She was educated. She was healthy. She did not overeat. For him to say she was getting too fat offended her. She was being careful since she lost one child already. He then advised her to get plenty of bedrest.

Betz laughed when one of the older patients warned her to never reach above her head, that it was unhealthy for the baby. That same lady told her to take a car ride on a bumpy road if she went past her due date. "It will induce contractions," she said. Betz understood these were old wives' tales, but listened to her ramble on without taking much notice of what she was saying.

Betz was thrilled. She was only one month away from completing her training as a nursing assistant. She felt fortunate to have the ability to continue her education throughout her pregnancy. She had been worried they may kick her out of the program once they found out she was expecting, but they hadn't. They let her continue.

With no family to help her, Betz understood her duty was to stay home with her child after giving birth. She would be unable to continue working as she hoped. One day, she vowed to use the skills she now possessed. It would not go to waste.

Evelyn came, staying for the weekend. The two women were celebrating the end of Betz's training. Ham, mashed potatoes, and corn were served for dinner. An apple pie sat atop the cooling rack for dessert. Drinking white wine, Evelyn made a toast.

"To Betz and her accomplishments. She is now a nurse's aide. She is about to give birth to her first child. Cheers."

Betz raised her glass, acknowledging the toast her friend just gave. After clinking the two glasses together, they both took a sip.

They sat and chatted for hours, just like the old days. Exhausted, Betz stood and said good night. Evelyn followed her up the stairs to the guest bedroom she slept in when she came to stay.

Evelyn was in a deep, dreamlike sleep when a loud noise resounded throughout. It jolted her to an upright position. She listened attentively to see if it had been part of her dream. When the guttural sound came again, she ran to Betz's bedroom. She was holding onto the bedpost, trying to take deep breaths.

"The baby's coming." She yelled at Evelyn.

Evelyn sprang into action immediately. She helped Betz put on a house dress and shoes before running into her own room. She slipped on her clothes in record time. She heard Betz groaning with every contraction that came.

"Let's go." She shouted, not meaning to sound brusque.

Instead of replying, she began descending the stairs.

The scene taking place was comical. Betz, grasping the handrail as she waddled down the steps while Evelyn was one step ahead of her, ready to catch her if she fell forward. No way her petite frame could stop the pregnant mom if she stumbled.

Evelyn grabbed their handbags, keys to her car, and the suitcase standing in a corner by the entryway before slamming the door behind her. The contractions were becoming more frequent. Betz was worried they may not make it to the hospital in time. The baby was rushing to enter the world.

There was little traffic on the roads. It was the middle of the night. Not knowing how, they arrived at the Emergency ward before they knew it. Evelyn, experiencing nothing like this, ran around yelling at anyone and everyone. A wheelchair was brought to the door, taking Betz away. The *clip-clop* of Evelyn's heels was right behind her. She would not let her friend have this baby on her own.

Betz's eyes suddenly widened. "I need to push." She shouted at the nurse.

"Not yet," the nurse said.

"You don't understand. The baby's coming. NOW!"

When they reached the room, a team of four assisted Betz to the bed. There was a flurry of activity. Minutes later, Betz saw them whisk her baby away. She started to ask if anything was wrong, but a nurse was pressing hard on her abdomen. It took everything she had not to scream. Finally, the nurse stopped. The placenta had expelled itself. Everything happened so quickly, Betz felt delirious.

A nurse's aide began to sponge her body with warm water. Once completed, she helped her out of the clothes she arrived in, and into a hospital gown. Betz didn't have time to change since the baby came too quickly. Hospital protocol prevented her from seeing the baby until both were cleansed and put into fresh garments.

Flustered, Evelyn came to her bedside with a huge smile on her face.

"That was crazy," she said. "I can't believe how quickly she came."

Betz caught the words Evelyn said. She realized no one announced if she had a boy or a girl. "She?" she said in a questioning voice.

"Yes, it's a girl. Isn't that wonderful? They didn't kick me out. They were too busy with you. I stayed for the whole thing," Evelyn beaming, having witnessed the birth.

Betz craned her neck towards the door. She saw the nurse carrying her baby girl swaddled in a pink blanket with a pink bonnet on her head. The sun was just coming up. Outside, a vibrant red cardinal sat on the ledge of the window. It stayed there, not moving, sharing the moment Betz met her daughter for the first time.

When her baby was placed in her arms, Betz's face filled with wonder. A love unlike any other engulfed her.

Now, I understand what Mother was saying when she told me how much I meant to her. I didn't appreciate it before, but now I do. There is no stronger bond than a mother with her child.

Chapter 14

The morning was laden with apprehension and chaos as Betz left the hospital with Annie Elizabeth, a name chosen to honor both Anneliese and Kenneth's mother. Kenneth had written to her months before, hoping she'd accept his mother's offer of staying with her for a few days after the delivery. It was the best thing he could offer. Without her own mother to help, Betz reluctantly accepted. She sensed it'd put Kenneth at ease, knowing she was not going home alone with the baby.

Elizabeth Johnson was a nice enough lady, but her nervous energy made others on edge, including her daughter-in-law. Every time she called Betz during the pregnancy Betz hung up the phone exhausted. Her mother-in-law never relaxed. She worried about everything and it rubbed off on others. She meant well and was always willing to lend a helping hand.

The Johnsons arrived at the hospital later than the appointed time. Brimmer was a few hours' drive for them. Since they had driven there only one or two times before, they misjudged the traffic.

That was only the beginning. Elizabeth, eager to help, insisted Annie be wrapped in layers before they left. When she took her granddaughter away from Betz, Annie began to wail. This upset Elizabeth. A nurse kindly took over, ensuring everyone Annie was fine, her soothing demeanor calming everyone.

Once everyone was settled in the car, Donald, Kenneth's father, tried to ease the tension as he drove away from the hospital. His deep throated voice asking questions about his granddaughter, his wife sitting quietly beside him, listening intently for the answers. Betz told herself she could do this. It was only a couple of days.

After arriving at the house, Donald ensured things were in order before kissing his wife goodbye. He would return in three days. Elizabeth had her own household to run. Kenneth's younger brother and sister were still in school, so she couldn't stay long.

Elizabeth gave instructions to her husband as he walked out the door. He nodded his head, not listening. Betz smiled to herself. *Everyone may benefit from a few days away.* Then she chastised herself for thinking this about Kenneth's mother.

The next few days flew by rather quickly. Betz was surprised at how tired she was. Her labor had not been long, so she thought her recovery would be quick. Elizabeth suggested she rest during the day since she could attend to Annie's needs. Betz took advantage of her suggestion, amazed at how much it helped.

The two women took turns preparing bottles. The formula comprising of one can of evaporated milk mixed with water and corn syrup. Her mother-in-law gave Betz tips on how to prepare a bottle with one hand while holding Annie in the other. Elizabeth shared other tricks she learned over the years with her daughter-in-law.

Elizabeth took over the meal preparation. It had been a while since someone else cooked for Betz. She appreciated the break. Her mother-in-law put together several dinners, easy ones to heat after she left, when Betz was on her own. Betz was indebted to her for all her help.

In the evenings, after Annie was asleep for the night, they sat and talked. Betz enjoyed getting to know her mother-in-law more. One evening, Elizabeth surprised her by sharing her own childhood days.

"At an early age, I lost my mother. Since I was the eldest, I became responsible for my younger siblings. They relied on me for everything. I had no clue what I was doing. I constantly worried I was doing things wrong." Elizabeth, admitted. "I can't help myself. I worry about everything now."

Betz looked at Elizabeth differently. It all made sense now. Life's circumstances made it necessary for her to grow up fast. It molded her to who she was today. She had a huge responsibility on her shoulders at such a young age. No wonder she worried so much. It reminded Betz not to judge people so quickly.

Betz, encouraged by her mother-in-law's openness, shared with her the miscarriage she endured, her despondency over losing a child, and the depression she experienced. The guilt she felt over thinking she did something wrong. How she downplayed what happened to her son, not wanting him to worry.

Elizabeth shocked, hugged her daughter-in-law. "I'm so sorry this happened to you. I'm sorry you were alone."

The next evening, Betz told Elizabeth about her search for her father.

"Some people may think I'm obsessed. Maybe I am. It's driving me mad not knowing my background, where I come from. What happened? Someday I hope to know," Betz said.

Elizabeth sympathized with her. "There were lots of things happening then; the war, The Great Depression. Who knows what happened to him?"

"I know. That's just it. I want to hear my story."

A fondness for each other grew during the days they spent together. After she left, Betz answered Elizabeth's questions in a kind and patient way whenever she called. There was a new respect for her mother-in-law.

Motherhood came easily for Betz. She was fortunate she only had the responsibility of her daughter. She spent her days with Annie lying on her chest, fast asleep, reading a book. Her baby's warm body against her own brought joy as she watched the soft breaths go in and out. It was hard to lay her down in her crib. When she saw Annie smile in her sleep, Betz had to hold in a laugh. Annie was a delightful baby. Mother and daughter bonded more each day.

Betz just finished reading 'A Tree Grows in Brooklyn' and was ready for another book. Her daughter in one arm, a bottle in her other, Betz tried grabbing one off the shelf in the office. The book next to it fell to the floor. Setting the bottle on the desk, she stooped over, grabbing it by its spine. A picture laid on the floor where the book had fallen. She picked it up, walking over to the window for a better view.

The young man in the photo was wearing a military uniform. She wondered who he was. She had seen lots of pictures of Frank. It wasn't him. She'd never seen this person before. Maybe it was a relative of her grandfather's. As she peered closer, she noticed the uniform was from WWI. She turned the picture over. There was nothing written on the back. Annie began to fuss, hungry, wanting to be fed. She'd get the photo albums down later to compare him to other family members. For now, she had a daughter who needed her attention.

Betz had a gift for writing. She described her everyday life whenever she wrote to Kenneth. She was very detailed in her storytelling. She did not want him to miss out on what their child was doing. She wanted to share those moments with him. No matter how untimely the letters were, Kenneth was overjoyed to receive the updates. It made him feel closer to home.

Annie proved to be a strong-willed child. It was not surprising, considering how she arrived in this world. She learned to roll over and crawl before the average child. She began babbling at an early age. She was a child ahead of her time. Betz was looking forward to introducing her to her father who would be home soon. *At least she knows who he is.*

There hadn't been time for Betz to continue searching for her father. She was alone raising a child. She thought about him, though, and often wondered; *would he be interested in learning he was a grandfather?* In her world, he would.

Chapter 15

Kenneth's flight home from South Korea was exhausting. It had been a long, grueling year. His time overseas was finally ending. A short trip back to Brimmer was granted before he completed his military duty. At least his feet would be on American soil.

He was excited to meet his daughter for the first time. He worried about her reaction to him. He was a stranger to her. Weariness overtaking him, he slept hard with the rumble of the plane acting as background noise. It'd be a couple of days before he'd arrive home. He needed the sleep.

All morning, Betz had difficulty containing her excitement. She dressed Annie with great care. She selected a pink polka dot dress for her daughter to wear. When she pulled the dress over Annie's head, she squealed with delight. Betz brushed her gorgeous strawberry blonde hair until it shown. She placed a pink ribbon matching her dress in her hair.

"That won't last long," Betz said, laughing as she watched her daughter pull on it.

It was a special day. Annie was meeting her father for the first time. Kenneth was arriving on the two o'clock bus. Nervous and excited to see her husband, Betz kissed her daughter on the forehead. Her daughter sensed the excitement, and laughed.

As usual, Betz arrived early. With Annie in her arms, they waited at the bus stop. When Betz caught sight of it, she tightened her grip on Annie, making her screech. The bus came to an abrupt halt, throwing the passengers forward. The driver laughed when he opened the door.

"That should wake you up," he said.

Kenneth saw his wife holding his six-month-old baby standing there, waving. His parents next to her side. Tears welled in his eyes. He was back in Brimmer and there they were, waiting for him. The sight would make any grown man cry.

He stepped off the bus with eyes only on his family. Betz met him halfway, running into his outstretched arms. Kenneth engulfed them both, holding them tight. Annie squawked with delight. She sensed her mother's joy, and she loved hugs.

They heard the bus driver yelling.

"Please, everyone, collect your bags."

With hesitancy, Kenneth let his family go. He walked to where the baggage stood. He stopped to thank the bus driver and shake his hand.

"Thank you for your service," the bus driver said.

Kenneth grabbed his luggage, then hurried back to his wife and child. It had been a long year away. He missed them immensely. An indescribable ache no one understood.

Seeing Kenneth, Betz breathed a little easier. The danger of war was over. Soon, her husband would come home for good. His last month's serving in the military would be stateside at a US Marine base, a welcome relief from being overseas.

Kenneth spent his entire leave learning to be a father. Annie gravitated to him, not afraid as he feared she might be. His heart swelled with love. He never imagined having a child could bring this much joy. His sweet princess flooded his heart with emotions.

The Johnsons took advantage of their limited time together, enjoying life as a family. Betz and Kenneth relished being husband and wife again, appreciating the quiet moments they shared.

The time went too fast. Once again, Betz was saying goodbye to her husband. This time their daughter by her side. Annie sensed tension in the air. She didn't understand what was happening. She held her hands up to her Papa for him to take her into his arms. It nearly broke his heart. He kissed her forehead and told her to be good for her Mama.

He waved from the window as the bus pulled away.

The end was near. Their future was on the horizon.

Chapter 16

The following month, Betz took Annie to the cemetery. They had gone there several times before, but today was special. It was Anneliese's birthday. A bouquet of wildflowers was gripped in her child's hand. As they strode through the grass, Annie pointed to something lying on the ground. A big, white feather laid there. Excited, her daughter squirmed to get down, handing her mother the flowers she held. Betz laughed as Annie held onto her legs while reaching for the feather. She was learning to stand on her own, but still wobbly on her feet. Somehow, Annie grabbed a hold of the feather. She lost her grip, falling backwards. She looked up towards the sky, waving the feather, babbling incoherently. Betz wasn't sure what she saw or who she was talking to, but whatever it was, it made her child happy.

Betz picked her back up and continued walking. When they arrived near the gravesite, it did not surprise her to see the yellow rose lying there. She still didn't know the person's identity. She had come to grips with the fact she may never know.

Betz placed the bouquet of wildflowers next to the yellow rose. Annie, sitting on the ground twirled the feather in the air like a wand. Betz couldn't help but laugh. She turned back to the tombstone, saying, "I wish you were here to see your granddaughter. You'd spoil her more than she already is. Happy Birthday, Mother."

As they walked away, Betz said, "Say goodbye to your Nana." Annie complied by waving her hand back and forth.

"Nana would love you so much. She would have loved to have a granddaughter like you," Betz said.

In response, Annie tickled her mother's nose with the feather she held tightly in her hand as they walked back to the car.

One morning, while feeding Annie her breakfast, a rush of nauseousness came out of nowhere. Betz knew exactly what this was. She secretly hoped she'd become pregnant again when Kenneth was home on leave. Happy, her wish came true. This time, her husband would be home to witness the birth of their child. His military duty will have ended by the time the baby came. When he was home, they discussed having more children. As most fathers do, Kenneth wanted a boy, but Betz knew he'd be happy if it was another girl. She didn't care as long as nothing went wrong.

Time did not slow down. Annie was growing every day. She did things on her own schedule, the same way she entered the world. She learned to walk early. Her babble soon turned into words. She wanted to do things by herself, not wanting help. There was nothing stopping this child. She was a handful, knowing how to get her way. Her antics kept her mother amused. She was irresistible, a delightful child.

Grateful she no longer had to carry Annie around everywhere, Betz had a little freedom of her own. She was doing well with the pregnancy. The doctor reassured her things were going as planned.

A feverish anticipation filled the air the day Kenneth came home from the Marines. Betz planned a welcome home party despite the amount of work it took. His parents, siblings and friends were invited for an afternoon of food and drink. Stories of the war kept the guests longer than planned. No one seemed to mind. They finally left in the early evening hours.

Exhausted, but happy, the couple collapsed on the sofa with young Annie playing on the living room floor. Kenneth handed Betz a glass, toasting his safe arrival home. He leaned over and kissed his wife. Annie climbed on his lap, not wanting to be left out. He squeezed her tight.

He reached over and placed his hands on Betz's enormous belly. The baby made its presence known by kicking him. With a look of surprise on his face, he laughed. He was thankful he was here to experience this.

A few days later, Kenneth visited the Bailey Oil Company. The chance to earn more money as a driver was upmost on his mind. He sought information regarding the purchase of his own rig. A truck that delivered fuel to various locations. He was determined to achieve his goal.

One evening, after Annie was asleep, he was ready to broach the subject.

After describing his plan, he said, "I know it's a significant investment. I'm confident I can earn it back quickly, especially if offered more shifts."

Betz listened to the details. Kenneth had done the research and had it all worked out. He would seldom be gone overnight, and his potential salary would be significantly more than his earnings were before he was drafted.

"It's your money. It's your decision. If I doubted this venture for a second, I would never suggest it," he said, trying to convince her.

She waved a dismissive hand. "Shh, don't say that. It's our money. I trust you. If you think we should do it, then do it," she said. "We'll go to the bank tomorrow."

His lips curved into a smile. "This is right for our family. I know it is."

Kenneth left the house on his search to buy his new rig. He was like a kid wandering through a candy store. He scrutinized different truck setups before focusing on the one Ford offered. It had enough torque to pull a loaded tanker trailer from the terminals in Wisconsin and Iowa, the routes he'd be assigned to.

He settled on a bright red cab. It matched the gas trailer Bailey Oil Co. provided at their cost. He thought the color would look slick.

They were using Betz's inheritance money to buy the cab. They agreed to pay cash, preferring no payments. It was an enormous investment, taking a large chunk of money to purchase it. Kenneth was not worried. He promised to replenish the account with the extra money he made.

After Kenneth signed the purchase to buy papers, he climbed in the cab and pulled out of the Ford garage, sporting a big smile. He headed back to

Brimmer, eager to show his new baby to Betz. When he pulled into the driveway, he hit the air-horn, startling the neighborhood, including Betz and Annie. They ran to the door, wondering what was happening. Out stepped Kenneth from the cab, beaming with pride.

"Ain't she something, Betz? I can't wait to hook her up and begin driving for Bailey. Don't you just love the color? Gotta love the horsepower this baby puts out. It's incredible." He was talking a mile a minute.

Betz saw his excitement, complimenting him on his selection.

"You still need to get insurance and licensing, don't you?" she asked.

"I'm headed to Becker Insurance next. The dealership took care of the licensing for me," he said. "I'm driving over and leaving it at Chick's so he can work his magic on the lettering."

Chick was well known in the area for his artistic creativity. He was featured on billboards, business walls and signage all around town. Everyone knew Chick. He specialized in lettering business trucks and delivery vans. Kenneth was confident Chick would do a super job on his own rig.

A few days later, Chick called, telling Kenneth his semi cab was ready to pick up. Kenneth, pulled into Chick's shop and saw his big rig out front waiting for him.

Chick approached Kenneth and asked, "Well, what do you think?"

"Wow, it turned out great," Kenneth said. "The white lettering really stands out against the red background. I love it. You did a great job, Chick."

On closer inspection, Kenneth said, "Hey, man, you misspelled my name on the driver's door. It says Kenny instead of Kenneth."

Chick started laughing. "Don't you remember?" He reminded Kenneth of the story.

The two played together on a fast-pitch softball team a few years ago. After one game, and after a few beers, they started telling stories. One player gave Kenneth a hard time after making three errors in one game. He kept referring to him as Kenny.

"Remember how pissed off you got?" Chick said. "We laughed it off, and drank more beers."

"Oh yeah. I remember that. I was aware everyone was laughing at me. I guess Kenny will work. It's a reminder of the good times we had playing ball. You are something else, Chick."

As Kenneth opened the cab door, Chick yelled to him.

"Hey, I have some good news that may soften the shock of seeing the name Kenny on your truck. Bailey called. He's willing to pay for the lettering. I'm sending the bill to him."

"That's great news," Kenneth said. "The guys I work for are fantastic. They're always willing to help a guy out in a pinch."

Soon after, Kenneth began his career as a truck driver, returning each evening to his wife and child. He was happy. Life was good.

Chapter 17

Will Joseph Johnson was born without complications. His father, looking through the nursery window, was overcome with emotions, proud to have a son. Overjoyed for his family and the life they made together.

Routine became their norm. Kenneth left in the early morning hours to drive his truck route. Most days, he returned home by dinnertime, enjoying the rest of the evening with his family.

It was difficult maintaining order in the house with two young children, but Betz managed. The current task at hand was getting Will potty trained. Annie, playing mother, tried to assist, making it ten times harder.

It was almost summer. Betz was looking forward to the warmer evenings. It had been a cold and wet spring.

Kenneth was in Iowa with an overnight haul. Betz, half asleep, heard Will crying out. Dazed from sleep, she went to comfort him. When she entered his room, she saw him tossing and turning amongst the covers; the blankets twisted around his small body from the movements. She placed her hand on his forehead. He was burning up. She hurried to the bathroom for a cold compress. She placed it on his feverish head.

"Poor baby. You don't feel good, do you?" Betz asked.

Will shook his head no.

Betz noticed he was having difficulty swallowing. Bringing him a glass of water, she watched as he tried to drink.

"I so tired, Mama," he said.

"Go to sleep, darling. I'll stay right here with you."

Betz could not stop herself from worrying as she sat by his side. Her experience as a nursing assistant was kicking in. She prayed it was not what she thought it might be. The poliovirus had hit several communities. It would be terrible if her little Will contracted it. She'd take him to the clinic tomorrow. No matter what, she needed to keep Annie away from him.

Will slept until noon the following day. Betz chose not to wake him, knowing the rest would do him well. Besides, she had to figure out a plan. Kenneth would not be home until late, and she had Annie to worry about.

Not knowing what else to do, she called Kenneth's mother. "I understand this is a lot to ask, but can Annie please come stay with you? Will is very sick. I don't want her to become ill as well. Kenneth will not arrive home until early evening. I'll ask him to meet you halfway tomorrow, if that works for you."

"Oh, Betz, poor Will. Annie can stay with us as long as you need."

Before Elizabeth began asking more questions, Betz thanked her, saying she had to go.

Betz was never happier seeing her husband walk through the door that night. Her hands full all day long, trying to keep Annie occupied while attending to Will's care. She needed his help. Kenneth immediately ran to Will's room to see his son. Standing in the doorway, he could tell his little boy was not doing well. Tears welled in his eyes. He felt helpless.

"I'm sorry I wasn't here, Betz," he said.

"It's not your fault." She tried reassuring him.

She explained the plans to take Annie to his parents' house the next day.

"I didn't know what other choices I had." Her tone defensive.

"You did the right thing. Mom will take care of her while you nurse Will back to health."

Kenneth left with Annie early the next morning. She sensed something was wrong, but did not ask questions. She loved her grandparents. She had never stayed overnight by herself. Mama said it would be an adventure. She was excited.

When Kenneth returned home, they wrapped Will in a blanket. It was warm outside, but Betz preferred leaving nothing to chance. They drove to the doctor's office in silence. Apprehensively, they sat waiting for the nurse to call their name.

The doctor asked questions, examined Will, and drew blood from him. The blood test would confirm the diagnosis, but he firmly believed it was polio. He had seen several cases lately.

Kenneth asked about recovery.

The doctor explained each case was different. Will's prognosis was uncertain at the moment. He explained there were a lot of unknowns with this disease, and gave instructions for his care. The doctor wanted to see him again if he worsened. He assured them he'd call as soon as he got the test results back. He reminded them Will was contagious for the next two weeks. They should do their best to keep others away. They assured him they would.

Betz gripped the phone tighter when the clinic called to confirm the diagnosis. The poliovirus was the culprit for her son's illness. At least they knew what they were dealing with.

The headache, sore throat, fever and tiredness worsened over the course of three weeks. Betz's nursing skills came in handy. It was difficult getting him to eat. He kept telling her it did not taste good. She tried everything. No matter what she gave him, he barely ate anything.

It was a relief when the symptoms began to decrease. Betz became hopeful the end was near.

Annie came home after Will was no longer contagious. She was rambunctious. A welcome change from the quiet solitude they had been living under. Betz worried it was too much for her son, still trying to recover. Will adored his sister and was glad she was home. Annie laid in bed with him, quietly talking, making him smile. She sang nursery rhymes to him until he fell asleep. Her grandmother, constantly worrying, warned her to be a good girl when she got home. She loved her little brother. She would help any way she could.

It was the Fourth of July. Will was feeling better with no more cough or fever. Betz thought it time he enjoyed the outdoors, to feel the sunshine on his face. Happy to leave the house, Will was excited to dress in regular clothes. Betz noticed how weak his little legs were when placing them into his pants. Not wanting to panic, she called for Kenneth.

"Dear, can you please carry Will to the porch?" she asked.

He scooped his son up in his arms and set him on the porch swing. He placed a blanket around his knees, sitting next to him. Will watched his little sister in the yard, running with the neighborhood kids, hair flying. He wanted to run with them, but when he stood up, his legs went to mush.

"It's too soon, Bud. You've been lying in bed for a long time. You have not used your muscles." Not completely understanding, he flexed his arm muscles to show his dad how strong he was. Kenneth laughed.

"I'll be right back. I'll get us something cold to drink," he said.

He wondered what was taking Betz so long to come outside to join them. He found her in their bedroom, sobbing.

"What's wrong?"

"It's Will. He can't use his legs," she said, crying.

"It'll take time. He hasn't used them in a long time."

"No, Kenneth. It's not just that. Did you see his legs? It is everything I feared. He has paralytic polio. The worst type anyone can have."

Stunned, Kenneth, not knowing how to respond, held his wife in his arms as she cried.

We cannot lose another child.

Chapter 18

Will's legs had no muscle strength to keep him upright. He was paralyzed. The child needed to be carried everywhere. He had no energy, still eating little. Most of his time, he spent lying in bed, playing with his toy trucks, surrounded by hot water packs placed on his legs.

Betz became obsessed, reading everything she could about polio. She visited multiple doctors, asking their opinions about therapies. She would not accept the idea this may be a permanent condition for her son. She was going to do everything in her power to help him overcome his disability.

Massaging the muscles in Will's legs became routine. Betz recited nursery rhymes, told stories, and sang songs to take his mind off what she was doing. When his legs were not being massaged, they kept them wrapped in warm towels or hot water bottles. Each night, she drew a hot bath for him, placing him in the hot water to soak. Articles written indicated hot water could do wonders for muscles. She was trying everything possible.

Kenneth was worried for his wife. He saw the exhaustion on her face when he arrived home each night. He wanted to help more, but also needed to work. The investment made in the semi-truck was significant. They needed his salary. He, too, was worn out, helping wherever, whenever he could. He wasn't sure how long they could keep this pace up. They needed help.

The summer flew by. Fall was upon them before they knew it. With the cooler weather, Betz sensed Will was getting stronger. It had been four long months since he had walked. One morning, while changing into his nightclothes, she noticed him hanging onto the edge of the bed, his legs showing more strength. She let him stand longer than usual, thinking it was building stamina. Each time, he stood longer and longer. When she showed Kenneth one evening, tears threatened to overtake them both. Their son was progressing. There was hope building.

At the next clinic visit, they impressed the staff with the headway Will was making. He could walk, but only if he had someone or something to hang onto. Betz asked a ton of questions. She wanted recommendations for leg braces, understanding Will needed a specialist for proper fitting. Dr. Nelson at Mayo Clinic was the physician suggested.

They planned a trip to Minnesota the following month. Kenneth's folks lived on their way to Rochester. They would drop Annie off with them while they visited with the doctor. Kenneth was taking a few days off to travel with them. No way would he allow his wife to travel that distance by herself, especially with two young kids. Plus, he wanted to hear firsthand what could be done for his son.

On the drive, Betz pointed out objects along the road, asking Will to repeat the words to her. She worried he was missing out, being cooped up in the house as long as he was. Enthusiasm to be outside, traveling across the state, was contagious among mother and son. It became an adventurous learning trip, and for a brief time, their worries were forgotten.

Staff in white coats were everywhere when they entered the enormous clinic. Nervous, but hopeful, they waited. It seemed like it took forever. Dr. Nelson's nurse finally called their name. She greeted them warmly, asking questions about Will's health history, their family history, the onset of the disease, the course it took, and how it progressed. Will had his temperature and vitals taken. Once completed, she told them Dr. Nelson would be in shortly.

The appointment was informative. Dr. Nelson said Will was a lucky young man. Many children with paralytic polio died when the muscles in their lungs became affected. He complimented Betz on her fortitude and dedication to treating Will. Pleased to learn Betz had a nursing background, he told them it would make the next steps easier.

Dr. Nelson took measurements of Will's legs, explaining how the braces worked. They stabilized the child, allowing him to build more strength, giving him independence to do things by himself. He warned them it may be costly. It would require several trips to Mayo. He personally would follow Will and track his progression.

The cost didn't matter to the Johnsons. They wanted whatever was best for their son.

Dr. Nelson asked them to return in two weeks to receive the braces.

It was late when the appointment ended. They rented a hotel room, not wanting to drive back in the dark. After tucking Will into bed, they talked about their finances. The amount of money needed to give Will the best chance for recovery was unknown. It wasn't just the cost for medical treatment, but the number of trips to Mayo. They couldn't make it in one day. Each trip would require an overnight stay. The cost would add up.

Betz was adamant she did not care about the cost. They'd use the money she inherited. They already spent a large amount to purchase the truck Kenneth was driving. They'd need to evaluate what was remaining. At least they owned the house. Kenneth said he could work extra shifts if he had to. They agreed, giving their son what he needed was their priority. Everything else was secondary.

The braces for Will worked. They helped maintain his balance, giving him the ability to walk without help. As he grew, it became necessary to be refitted with different braces time and time again. The trips to Mayo Clinic became tedious and costly, but Dr. Nelson was wonderful. The Johnsons were doing everything they could to improve Will's life, even though it ate into their savings.

Shortly after, the polio vaccine became a standard vaccine for children. It came a little too late for Will Johnson. The effects of his affliction with the poliovirus remained with him his entire life.

Chapter 19

Annie sat on the bedroom floor, playing with her dolls, pretending to be a nurse taking care of her patient. It was too cold to go outside. Her mother was with Will. Mama spent a lot of time in Will's room, keeping his legs warm. She was never to interrupt Mama unless it was really important whenever she tended to her brother.

Her stomach growled. She was hungry. She wandered downstairs to find food. She pulled a chair closer to the counter, and climbed on top to reach for the cookie jar. She snuck a handful of cookies before hurrying back upstairs to her room. Her mother would disapprove of eating cookies before lunchtime, but they tasted so good. Besides, she was always busy with Will.

She wished it was still summer. At least then, she could go outside and play with the neighbor kids. Now, she was stuck in her room, playing by herself until lunch was ready. She loved lunch time. It was her special time with Mama. They sang songs and sometimes even danced around the kitchen. She loved it when they acted silly, making her giggle until sometimes she got the hiccups. Mama told her how proud she was of her for being a big girl while Mama was preoccupied with her little brother. Those words meant the world to her. They made up for the times she spent alone.

In the afternoon, she got to sit beside her brother in his bed, playing make believe. Annie, having quite the imagination, talked about faraway places and people they had yet to meet. She enchanted Will with the stories she weaved. Betz smiled, seeing the two of them together. She heard Annie telling Will the things they'd do when he got better. Annie was wonderful with Will. He adored his big sister.

In the evenings, Papa tried teaching her the game of checkers. She became frustrated when she made a wrong move, but Papa was patient with her, explaining what she did wrong. She didn't always win, but when she did, her papa beamed at her with excitement. He and Mama took turns tucking her in for the night. When it was Papa's turn, he let her choose a storybook to read. When it was Mama's turn, she'd tell stories of magical faraway places. She often dreamed of living there one day.

Annie became used to getting dropped off at her grandparents' house after driving for hours in the car. Her parents continued the trip without her to attend Will's doctor appointments. The first couple of times she stayed, it was exciting and fun. Her grandmother, Elizabeth, spent time with her, spoiling her, giving her whatever she asked. When her Aunt Donna and Uncle Bruce came home from school, they were excited to see her and gave her the attention she desired.

Farm work didn't stop, even though a little one was visiting. Aunt Donna and Uncle Bruce had chores to do. Soon, Annie was assigned her own jobs whenever she visited. At first, she was afraid to go to the chicken house, but Aunt Donna showed her how to gather eggs lying underneath the hens. They were fragile, so she needed to be careful not to break them. Soon, she was doing it by herself, no longer worried the chickens would peck her. She started naming them, making them less terrifying. Grandpa Donald was proud of his granddaughter for her fearlessness and her adaptability.

After dinner, Aunt Donna often entertained her in her room. Her aunt was in high school and she loved the teenage clothes, so different from Mama's. One evening, Aunt Donna sat her on the bed and applied make-up to her face. When she looked in the mirror, it surprised her how grown-up she looked. She couldn't wait to be older, like her aunt.

Annie remembered the day Will came home with braces on his legs.

"Honey, Will can go outside and play with you. Isn't it wonderful?" Mama said, holding back tears. It was, indeed.

Annie began school the following year. She was more than ready. She learned how to take care of herself during Will's illness, and she loved adventures. Throughout the years, Betz was told repeatedly by Annie's teachers, her daughter was older than her years. She was fearless, never afraid to try things.

As a mother, she realized polio had not just affected her son. It shaped the life of her daughter, as well. She wondered what the future would hold for both of them.

Chapter 20

The family was going through a lot. Both kids were forced to stay indoors more than kids should. It was beyond their control, so the Johnsons splurged. The kids were delighted when Kenneth surprised them with an RCA Victor color television set. Something the entire family could enjoy.

On Saturday, they invited Evelyn and Stuart, recent newlyweds, to see their purchase. When they turned on the television, everyone gathered around, transfixed by the screen. The picture wasn't the greatest, but it was in color. No one complained.

Betz was happy for Evelyn. Their recent wedding was a festive day filled with lots of food and drink. Betz stood by her friend as Matron of Honor. She enjoyed every minute of that day, with one exception. A moment of regret overcame her as she watched Mr. Wilcox walk his daughter down the aisle. It reminded her of the promise she made to herself to discover her own father's identity. Life often impeded one's goals. One day, she would search again. For now, he remained an image in her mind.

Stuart brought over the plans for the house they were building in Lansbury. Kenneth was impressed with the layout. They were working with Mr. Connolly, one of the owners at the local lumber store in town. He was helping them calculate the correct amount of building supplies they needed.

"He really knows his stuff," Stuart said. "I would be lost without his help."

Stuart was planning on doing most of the work himself, having experience in construction. He told Kenneth he was unsure how long it would take him to build, but it was saving them a lot of money, by doing his own contracting.

To be courteous, Kenneth offered his help. He had little free time, but wanted to offer anyway.

The women went to check on the kids, leaving the husbands to their discussions. Evelyn confided in her that she was trying to become pregnant. Betz said nothing. She wondered why she was in such a hurry. *Shouldn't she wait until they completed the house?* she wondered. But then, admonished herself for thinking this. She remembered how much she wanted a child right after she and Kenneth married.

Betz, herself, was having difficulty getting pregnant again. It wasn't like she was trying to conceive she just wasn't doing anything to prevent it. A part of her wanted more children, but Will's illness made her question her dream of having a houseful of kids. She didn't think she could bear going through that again. She wondered if subconsciously her worry prevented her from becoming pregnant. Maybe deep down, she didn't want more children. It was too painful to feel helpless when they needed you the most.

By the end of the year, Evelyn and Stuart moved into their new house. To celebrate, they hosted a party for family, friends and acquaintances. The Johnsons arrived late. Kenneth had an unavoidable issue with one of the fuels stops.

Stuart, greeting them at the door, thrust drinks into their hands.

"Sorry, we're late," Kenneth said.

"No problem, buddy. Too bad though. I wanted to introduce you to Mr. Connolly. He's just getting in his car. Without him, this house would have taken another six months," Stuart said.

The Johnsons watched as the car drove away.

"Oh, well, your paths will most likely cross sometime," Stuart said, as they walked into the house to join the rest of the party.

Chapter 21

The years blended together, Kenneth and Betz dedicating their lives providing for their children in their different ways. Their love for each other never wavering even during the difficult times.

Visits with Evelyn and Stuart were frequent. Even though their children were younger than the Johnsons, they all got along splendidly. In the summer, the two families vacationed together on their favorite lake. Life in the fifties was good.

The teachers consistently told Betz Annie could earn better grades if she just tried a little harder. It was difficult getting her to stay on task long enough to complete her assignments, let alone be precise. Her interest was music and art. Areas she excelled in. She didn't care about anything else.

Betz remembered the moment she realized her daughter had talent. It was during a grade school performance when Annie played one of the four women who prepared the first Thanksgiving feast. Not wanting to be out-shown by the boy playing William Bradford, her voice boomed when reciting her rehearsed lines. She smiled directly at the audience as she served food to the pilgrims and their Indian guests. The audience erupted in laughter. The attention she received delighted her. The excitement she exhibited when they got home did not go unnoticed by her parents.

At the Christmas programs, her voice resounded above all the others. Her sweet, melodic range was a joy to the music teacher, never having someone so young have a voice so beautiful. The compliments Annie received made her beam. Betz and Kenneth were proud of their daughter.

Annie was a fierce big sister, protecting her brother whenever needed. Not that Will needed her help. He was managing well on his own. The braces helped immensely. He was getting stronger each day. By the time he turned eight, Dr. Nelson announced the braces were no longer necessary. Great news for the Johnsons. No more traveling to Mayo. Will could finally do things with his father he only dreamed about.

Opposite of his sister, school came easily to Will. He didn't have to try very hard to get good grades. Betz often thought it was due to all the time he spent lying in bed as a young child. She read him plenty of books and they played games all the time. He was unable to take part in outdoor activities like other kids, so reading passed the time.

Will had a harder time making friends. While his sister was outgoing and had lots of friends, he was quiet and preferred being by himself. The two siblings, remarkably different.

Betz volunteered at the hospital one day a week, giving her something to do besides run the household and taking care of the children. It seemed forever ago since she was a nursing assistant, helping wherever she could. She loved that time in her life, and was happy to be back doing something she loved.

One day, she ran into her mother's old acquaintance, Nurse Mae Wilson. They exchanged pleasantries and Mae asked to join her for lunch. Betz readily agreed. They grabbed a tray from the stack, waiting their turn in line, when Betz had a thought, she couldn't let go.

They sat at a table by the window overlooking the parking lot. Betz couldn't help herself. "Mae, how well did you know my mother?"

"Not well, but well enough," she responded.

She blurted out. "Do you know who my father is?"

Surprised at the question, Mae said, "Well, dear. I can't say I was close enough to your mother for her to confide in me. However, there were rumors."

"What rumors? Please, tell me what you've heard."

"The gossip was she was seeing a man from Lansbury. I never heard a name. They had broken up before anyone knew she was pregnant."

"Thank you. That's more than I knew."

"Now, Betz, I must remind you this was only rumors. I'm not sure if it's true."

"That's ok. It gives me another place to look," she said.

Mae quickly changed the subject. They continued chatting until they finished eating. Betz was reeling from the information she just heard. When she looked out the window, she watched the snow falling from the sky, hitting the ground.

By the time she finished her shift, snow covered the roads. She drove to the school waiting for the bell to ring, releasing the kids for the afternoon. Annie and Will hopped in the car, talking nonstop on the way home. With the abundance of snow on the ground, they planned on making a snowman when they got home.

Betz struggled to see through the windshield, and was relieved when she finally pulled into the driveway. *Whew! Safe and sound,* she thought to herself. Her heart hammering in her chest as she shut off the engine. She was grateful to be home, out of the storm.

Chapter 22

Kenneth was eager to get an early start to the day. He was driving his longest route today, and he wanted to get home at a decent hour. Before heading downstairs, he slipped into each of the children's rooms and kissed them on the forehead. "I love you," he said. "Never forget it." He whispered in each child's ear. "Be good for your Mama." They were oblivious, still sound asleep.

In the kitchen, he smelled the coffee brewing. Betz had breakfast ready and waiting. Whenever he ate a big breakfast, it allowed him an extra hour of driving, not taking time to stop and eat lunch. After devouring ham and eggs, he put coffee in his thermos before grabbing his wife in his arms. "I'm one lucky man," he said as he kissed her goodbye, walking out the door. "See you tonight."

"Wait." She teased him with another kiss before handing him a brown paper bag. "Something for the road."

The snow fell lightly to the ground when Kenneth hopped into the semi and began driving away from Brimmer. The forecast predicted an inch or two of light snow with heavier snowfall during the evening hours. He would be home before the worst came.

When Kenneth crossed the Iowa border, the snow was coming down harder. He still made decent time, arriving at his destination early. Relieved to have a break, he opened the brown paper bag Betz handed to him before he left. His favorite cookies were inside. *What a woman,* he thought. While they filled his tanker for the return trip, he refilled his thermos with hot coffee, prepared for the drive home.

The engine started easily on the first attempt. Kenneth prided himself on keeping his truck running smoothly. Maintenance was the key, fixing things before they broke. He just had it serviced before the winter set in. He swung the semi onto the highway and headed back to Brimmer.

The snow was coming down harder now, forcing him to focus on the road. Thankful for the hot coffee, he took a sip, thinking about the fire blazing in the fireplace and his warm bed waiting for him. He hoped to be home before the kids' bedtime. He hated it when he could not ask them about their day. He sighed heavily as he shifted into lower gear. The slick roads making him slow down. He knew he would not make it in time for the kids tonight.

Traffic on the highway decreased as Kenneth continued driving through the snow. He was going at a slow, but steady pace. Rockway was the next town. After that, he'd hit the most challenging portion of the trip. Wild Cat Ridge was a cumbersome half mile hill climb, causing the best-natured trucker to use cuss words. It made them lose precious time even when the weather was good. In winter, it seemed infinitely worse.

Kenneth drove through the streets of Rockway, waving at the snow plow drivers clearing the roads. *What a job,* he thought to himself. The sun was starting to go down, becoming dusk as he began to climb the hill on Wild Cat Ridge.

Kenneth gripped the steering wheel tighter as the trailer swerved to the left. He shifted into lower gear. When he did so, he lost the power required to make the climb with his full load. When he tried to increase his speed, the semi lost traction and began sliding again. After several attempts at trying to gain momentum without sliding, he let out an expletive.

Dammit! he yelled as he banged his fists against the wheel. He had no choice. If he was going to make it to the top, he needed chains on his wheels. He pulled off the road as far as he could and shut the engine off. He buttoned up his jacket before opening the door. He jumped to the ground, walking to the back of the cab. The set of chains rested in the metal box amongst tools any truck driver may need. The chains were bulky and awkward to handle as he pulled them from the container.

Hoisting them over his shoulder, he dropped them on the ground along the right side of the truck. Grateful there was still some daylight left, he vigorously worked to ensure the chains were snugly fit around the wheel. Happy with the results, he stood up, stomped his feet several times, trying to get warmth back into his toes.

He climbed back into the cab to warm up before starting the other side. His hands were so cold, he could barely unscrew the cap off the thermos. The coffee was lukewarm, not hot enough to warm him. He drank a half cup, anyway, before leaving the cab once again.

He threw the second set of chains down by the left wheel. On his knees, he began placing the chains around the wheel with the heavy snow continuing to come down and the wind howling in his ears. He was struggling with the links. Grabbing a flashlight out of the box, he laid on his back, holding the light, trying to determine what was wrong. Why couldn't he get it connected?

He heard the engine of an oncoming truck as the final chain link snapped into position. He tugged, making sure it was secure. In an instant, an excruciating pain overcame him. His legs were on fire. He didn't know what just happened. He searched for the source of the pain when he saw blood gushing from his extremities before he passed out.

Chapter 23

Jack Watson held both hands on the wheel as he began his descent on Wild Cat Ridge. The roads were snow covered and icy, taking all his concentration. He had driven this route for years, and dreaded this section of the highway, especially in winter.

Halfway down the hill, he saw a flashing directional light. He could see a semi pulled off the road onto the shoulder in the opposite lane. He cautiously downshifted. His rig did not slide on the snow. A good sign. As he slowed down further, he saw headlights of another trucker coming up the hill, towards him. He heard shifting. The semi was trying to pick up speed to make the climb. Jack flashed his headlights to warn the approaching driver of the stalled vehicle on the shoulder of the road, the blowing snow making it hard to see.

Jack was still a short distance away. He slowed down further, giving the oncoming trucker ample road to bypass the parked vehicle. The transmission sounded again as the trucker shifted into higher gear just as his cab passed the parked truck. When he shifted, the jerking motion forced the trailer he was pulling to slide to the right. Jack gasped, not believing what he just witnessed. The trucker continued his ascent on Wild Cat Ridge, oblivious to what had just happened.

Beneath his wheels, Jack felt his own truck hit an icy patch on the road. His adrenaline was running high. He quickly got it under control, bringing it to a stop. Without thinking, he jumped out of his cab and ran across the road. He saw the blood first, the patch of snow turning red.

He kneeled down beside the man lying there. He was unconscious, bleeding profusely. Jack had seen the back wheels of the semi-trailer slide off the road. Apparently, it had run over the man's legs. Panicked, he ran back to his cab to retrieve a blanket he always kept there for emergencies. His mind was going a hundred miles an hour as he returned to the victim. His first instinct was to stop the bleeding. He took off his belt and tied it around one mangled leg. He looked around, but had nothing else to use for another tourniquet. He then wrapped both legs with the blanket as tight as possible, hoping he had done the right thing.

Within minutes of doing so, he saw headlights coming in his direction. *Please let it be help.* He jumped to the ground, skidding to the middle of the road, waving his hands above his head, flagging the motorist down.

A pickup truck stopped in front of him. Jack ran to the driver's side, out of breath. The driver asked what the problem was. Jack quickly explained the situation. Without waiting, the man hopped back into his truck and spun off. His farm was only two miles away. He'd phone the police from his house. Help was on the way.

Leroy, another trucker, began his descent down the hill with an empty load. Ahead, a man was standing in the middle of the road, signaling for help. Cautiously bringing his rig to a halt behind Jack's trailer, he shut off the engine, grabbing his hat and gloves simultaneously.

Leroy, in his sixties, moved slower than in years past. Today, you would never know it. He hurried across the road towards the man on his knees. When he got closer, he saw a man lying on his back with a blood-soaked blanket wrapped around his legs.

Jack turned to Leroy, quickly telling him what had happened.

"I don't think we should move him. We don't know what injuries he has," said Leroy. "Let's try to keep him as warm as we can."

Leroy went back to his truck and grabbed his own blanket. He snatched a tarp also, not sure what they'd use it for. Jack rummaged in the injured driver's rig, looking for anything to keep the man warm. He noticed a picture tucked into the visor above the driver's side. He grabbed it, not knowing why. Without moving him, they wrapped him in the items they gathered. Jack glanced down at the picture of a smiling family. He placed it in the man's gloved hands, folding them close to his heart. Jack knew a trucker's family was everything. It was the reason they drove thousands of miles each year.

Jack told Leroy to stay with the injured man. He went to his truck, grabbing the road flares from his emergency kit. He placed them strategically on the road, so everyone could see them through the snow.

He wasn't about to let another tragedy happen tonight.

Both men breathed easier when they heard the sirens. They looked at each other with resignation. Not knowing what else they could do for this poor man, they had stood, guarding his body from the elements, waiting for help to arrive. The flashing red lights of the police car were a welcome sight, the ambulance following close behind. Jack and Leroy stood aside grateful help was here.

One medic examined the body to see what other injuries they may be dealing with. Another checked for a pulse and heartbeat. He was alive, thanks to Jack's quick thinking. The blanket and belt around the legs had slowed down the blood loss. They all knew time was of the essence. With utmost care, they lifted him onto a gurney and placed him in the back of the ambulance.

"We're taking him to Iowa City Hospital." The medic informed them as he hopped into the back, slamming the doors shut.

Jack and Leroy watched the ambulance drive away. Captain Ferris walked to where they stood, looking through the billfold he held in his hand. He retrieved it from the man's pants pocket before they placed him in the ambulance. "Man is from Brimmer," he said. "I'll contact their police department to notify the family. Man's lucky to be alive, thanks to you." He turned to Jack. "Did you see anything?"

"I saw the whole thing," he quickly replied. Jack told Captain Ferris how the back of the trailer swerved off the road when the driver shifted to gain speed. "The rear tire of the trailer ran over the gentleman. By what I could tell, he was off the road far enough, putting chains on the wheels. I don't think the driver even knew what happened. He kept on driving."

"Did you catch any details of the truck?" Ferris asked. Hopeful, but doubtful he'd give him something to go on.

Somehow, in the chaos, Jack remembered the first three numbers of the license plate. "It was an Iowa plate with numbers beginning with 946. It had red lettering on the side of the trailer. I didn't catch the name. I was concentrating on getting numbers off the plate."

Leroy spoke up. "It was Kraemer Trucking." They both looked at him in disbelief.

"What?" he asked when he saw the look on their faces. "There aren't many trucks on the road tonight. It's a habit of mine to look at every truck I meet," he added.

Since the Captain had an eyewitness to the accident, there was no need to process the scene any further. He knew what happened.

Leroy suggested they take the injured man's fuel truck to Rockway.

"It's a hazard, leaving it here," he said.

The men agreed. Leroy volunteered to drive it. Once in the cab, he felt strange sitting in the seat of another man's truck, especially in this situation. With the chains on, Leroy managed the hill, driving the full load to Rockway with Captain Ferris following behind. He pulled the rig into the Piggly Wiggly parking lot.

Leroy looked around the cab, brushing his hand across the dash. "Sorry, man," he said out loud before climbing out. He locked the door, before getting into the police car. He handed the keys to Captain Ferris. Little was spoken on the trip back to his truck. A terrible accident just occurred, and both men were deep in their own thoughts.

Jack waited in his cab until Leroy returned.

Ferris thanked the two men for their help. He informed them they'd try to track down the guy who did this. The information they gave was helpful. He got back into his squad car and drove away.

Leroy told Jack he knew the injured man's name. "Kenneth Johnson from Brimmer, Wisconsin."

A name made it more real.

It had been quite the night. Both men were eager to get home but reluctant to leave. They just shared something horrific. After exchanging a few words, they walked away from each other, wishing each other safe travels.

Jack started his engine, pulling onto the road with caution. He kept playing everything over in his mind. A scene he'd rather forget, but knew it was impossible. *That could have easily been me.*

Chapter 24

Betz stood in the kitchen, waiting for the water to boil. She pulled back the curtains on the kitchen window. The snow was still falling outside. No doubt, Kenneth would not make it home before dinner tonight. She'd keep a plate warm for him. He appreciated a hot meal after a long day on the road.

When dinner was ready, she called the kids to the table. Will took a generous portion of ham and mashed potatoes. Annie, as usual took a much smaller portion. Little did her mother know, she'd sneak snacks to her room after school. By dinnertime, she was too full to eat much.

The talk around the table was lively. Annie, kept them entertained throughout the meal. She was always full of stories about school. Will, still quiet and soft-spoken, laughed at his sister's detailed description of everything she did.

Betz looked around her and smiled. She loved her children with all her heart. They were getting so grown up. She missed the fact they did not need her like they had. She treasured the age they were now. The dream of having lots of children did not come to fruition. The idea of having another child frightened her after one miscarriage and almost losing Will. She was content with the family she had.

After dinner was over, she instructed the children to complete their homework before they watched any television. Betz finished drying the last dish, taking off her apron when the doorbell rang. *Who could that be in this weather?* she wondered.

Will got to the door first. When he opened it, and saw who was standing there, he yelled, *Mom!*

As Betz approached the door, she saw Officer Fletcher whom she knew well, standing on her porch. Everyone around could hear the intake of her breath.

"Betz, may I come in?" he asked in a soft-spoken voice.

Betz stood aside, allowing Officer Fletcher walk past her into the foyer. For the first time, she noticed Eugene Young standing behind him. Eugene was a friend of Kenneth's. They became friends after Eugene started working at the Bailey Oil Company. Kenneth thought he was a good guy and worked hard.

What is he doing here?

Eugene stomped the snow off his boots before following the Officer into the house. Betz led them to the living room. She was shaking. She recalled another snowy night. The night a different officer came and told her mother, Dr. Miller, her soon to be fiancé, had died in a car accident.

Betz could barely breathe. Officer Fletcher removed his hat before speaking.

"Betz, there's been an accident. Kenneth has been taken to Iowa City Hospital. He's alive, but unconscious. He has massive injuries to his legs." He spoke quickly, not waiting for Betz's reaction. The Officer purposely did not give her the details of the accident, thinking now was not the time.

"Eugene's here to drive you to the hospital," he informed her.

Betz heard Will whimpering on the stairs. Annie was trying to hush him. When she heard the noise, she spun around. Disoriented, she looked at her children, then ran over, embracing them in her arms. "It'll be ok. It'll be ok," she repeated as if reassuring herself.

Officer Fletcher shook Eugene's hand before seeing himself out. They exchanged a look between them. They both understood Kenneth's chances for survival were not good. However, it wasn't their place to share this with Betz. Right now, she needed support. Eugene was here to do just that.

Eugene shifted from foot to foot, wanting to give Betz time to digest the news, but also knowing how important it was to get to the hospital. He gently prodded. "Betz, we better get going. It's a long drive."

Betz stood. "I need to call Kenneth's parents. I have to phone Evelyn to come watch the children," she said.

Annie stood in front of her mother and with a booming voice argued. "Mama, we're going with you. We need to be with Papa."

Betz began to disagree with her when Eugene stepped in.

"Betz, Kenneth will want them there. He will want to see them."

Straightening her back, she turned to Annie, saying, "You are too wise for a ten-year-old." Regaining her composure, she instructed the children to pack a small suitcase and put on warm clothes. She was unsure how long they would need to stay in Iowa City. It was better to be prepared, and it was a long trip back home.

Eugene volunteered to call Kenneth's parents and her friend Evelyn while Betz got herself ready. She agreed and rushed upstairs. An address book sat next to the telephone. He dialed the Johnson's phone number. Kenneth's father, Donald, answered. Eugene explained what happened. Donald let out an expletive unlike anything he heard before. He told Eugene to let Betz know they'd meet her in Iowa City.

Next, he called Evelyn. When she answered the phone, she was surprised to hear Eugene's voice. She knew him from gatherings they had been at together.

"Evelyn, I have bad news. Kenneth's been in a severe accident," Eugene said in an anguished voice.

Evelyn clutched the phone to her ear. She was trembling.

Eugene heard sobbing from the other end of the line. He waited.

Stuart, seeing Evelyn's reaction to the call, took the phone away from her.

"Who is this?" Stuart asked.

Eugene repeated the events of the evening.

Shocked by the news, Stuart thanked him for calling and hung up. He knew his wife. There was no question in his mind. He'd drive her to Iowa City where she was needed to support her friend.

Betz and the kids descended the stairs, suitcases in hand. Eugene quickly offered his help by taking them and setting them down on the floor. He already checked the back door, ensuring it was locked securely. He extinguished the flames in the fireplace, and walked room by room, checking to make sure the house could be left unoccupied for a few days.

Eugene took the luggage to the car, placing them in the trunk while the others donned coats, hats, and mittens. The kids climbed into the backseat of his 1957 Ford Fairlane. He walked back to the porch, taking the key from Betz's trembling hands. He locked the front door behind them. He opened the passenger door for Betz before hurrying around, and slipping into the driver's seat. He looked back at the children, and noticed Annie's arms around her brother. He looked sideways at Betz, seeing her tense body before turning the key in the ignition. The sound of the engine broke the silence. Eugene eased the car onto the main road. It was still snowing. He had a man's family in his care tonight. Caution was utmost on his mind.

It didn't take long for the children to fall asleep. When they crossed the Iowa border, the snow became heavier. Eugene concentrated on his driving. Betz was deep in her own thoughts, silently praying Kenneth would be awake when she arrived, teasing her for coming all this way for nothing. When they neared Iowa City, Eugene was glad to see the roads plowed, allowing them to pick up more speed.

Finally, the car pulled into the entrance to the hospital. Kenneth stopped the car, letting Betz and the children out before parking the car in the visitors' parking lot. He hated the thought of them going in alone, but he had no choice. He had to park the car.

Betz stopped at the reception desk, identifying herself. She told them her husband was brought in by ambulance a few hours ago. They scanned their lists of patients. Once they located his name, they gave directions to the ward Kenneth was on.

Fortunately, Eugene found a close place to park. Not surprising on a night like tonight. He hurried inside, and noticed Betz standing by the elevators. He jaunted over to them before the doors opened. Ushering them inside, he gave his friend's wife's hand a squeeze. Betz welcomed the unspoken words of encouragement. The light lit up when Will pushed the button on the elevator panel. He held his tummy as the elevator lurched upwards, looking at his Mama with surprise. Instinctively, she grabbed his hand and pulled him closer to her side.

The elevator door opened on Kenneth's floor. Dread overcame Betz when she realized they were on the critical care floor. The beeping machines pounding in her head, she walked to the nurses' station with the children close behind. When she identified herself, the nurse immediately dropped her head, but not before Betz caught the sorrow in her eyes. *Please, please*, she silently prayed.

"I'll page the doctor. He'll be right with you," she informed them.

Betz wanted to scream. *Just let me see my husband*, but remained silent.

Within minutes, the doctor approached her. Without mincing words, in a matter-of-fact voice, he told her Kenneth's injuries were severe. He had a lot of blood loss. He was unconscious and had not woken up since they brought him in. His condition was grave, and the next twenty-four hours were critical.

Betz took a big shuddering breath and asked if she could see him. The doctor agreed, but suggested she go in alone, without the children. She turned to Eugene, pleading with her eyes. Immediately, Eugene stepped in. He asked the kids if they wanted a hot chocolate after the long drive. At first, they refused. They did not want to leave their Mama, but when enticed by other goodies, they relented. Eugene led the way to the cafeteria as Betz trailed behind the doctor.

She followed the Doctor to the other side of the ward. Before he let her enter, he reminded her how crucial the next few hours were. Tears welled in her eyes, understanding the underlying meaning of his words.

When the curtain was pulled back, she let out a low moan. Shocked at seeing her husband lying in the hospital bed, looking as he did. She expected to see the tubes, monitors and dressings. It was the deathlike pallor of his face that surprised her. Not being able to hold back her tears any longer, she bent over the bed and kissed him. She brushed his hair back from his forehead and pressed her cheek against it. The love she had for him came pouring forth, telling him she loved him and what he meant to her. She stroked his arm, hoping he sensed her presence.

A nurse walked in, apologizing for the interruption.

"It's time to take his vitals and check the pulse at his extremities," she told Betz.

Betz watched as she checked his vitals. When the nurse pulled back the blankets covering Kenneth's legs, she grabbed for the nearest chair. Overcome by a sick feeling in the pit of her stomach, she continued to stare. The extent of his injuries, now a reality.

Oh My God! Oh My God! Oh My God! What in the hell happened?

She realized then she had not been told the details of the accident. It was much worse than she thought.

Betz managed to pull herself together. Her experience as a nurse's aide, taking over. She asked questions beyond what a typical wife of a patient would ask. Once she explained her background as a nursing assistant, Margaret, the nurse, explained Kenneth's extensive crush injuries in more detail.

"I was here when they brought him in," she explained. We stabilized him, but the blood loss was significant. It was touch and go for a couple of hours."

"His skin is cold and clammy. He's so pale," Betz said, placing her fingers on his wrist. "His pulse is weak. These are not good signs."

"Unfortunately, no, they are not. We'll know more by tomorrow if…"

Margaret did not finish the sentence. There was no need. Betz finished it for her, but not aloud. *If he made it until tomorrow.*

Eugene and the children were returning from the cafeteria when they bumped into Evelyn and Stuart. Will ran up to Evelyn, hugging her around the legs. "Papa got hurt," he cried.

"I know, darling boy. I know." A worried look between Eugene and Evelyn did not go unnoticed by Annie.

They returned together to the waiting room near the critical care unit. The men remained with the kids while Evelyn sought Betz out. She wanted her friend to know she arrived. When Betz saw Evelyn standing in the doorway, she ran to her, collapsing in her arms. Evelyn rubbed her back, trying to soothe her.

"It's not good." Betz tearfully told her.

Betz grabbed Evelyn's hand, leading her into Kenneth's room. Evelyn saw him lying there, looking white as a ghost, with eyes closed. It was difficult to keep herself together. She grabbed and hugged her friend, not saying a word. The devastation she felt left her speechless.

Betz turned towards the bed. "Look who's come to see you? It's Evelyn." She waved Evelyn over closer to where she stood.

Surprised by this exchange, Evelyn, following Betz's lead, greeted Kenneth as if awake. After a few minutes of pleasantries, Betz motioned her friend to the doorway to explain.

"For the children's sake, we are going to pretend Kenneth can hear us, like he's in a deep sleep. The kids need to see him. I think the sooner, the better. Can you wait here until I bring them in? I don't want him to be alone."

Now that Evelyn understood Betz's perspective, she sat in the chair alongside Kenneth's bed, talking about nonsensical things. Things Kenneth would laugh at if he could actually hear her speaking.

As Betz made her way towards the lounge area, Dr. Mertz stopped her. "Mrs. Johnson. Your husband's vitals are not improving. He has a rapid heartbeat and his pulse is weak. I'm sorry. We will continue to monitor him closely, but his chances of making it through the night are slim."

Betz knew what he was saying was true, but having it put into words was hard to comprehend. Her face turned pale. She thought she was about to faint, her breathing becoming erratic. Dr. Mertz saw she was hyperventilating, signaling for help. They made her sit on the nearest chair, and told her to put her head between her knees. It helped. She apologized for her reaction, assuring them she was fine. Someone handed her a glass of water before letting her stand. She reassured them again she was alright. Betz rushed to where her children sat drawing pictures.

Annie saw her first. She ran to her mother with tears in her eyes. *The grownups were all so stupid. They didn't think she understood what was happening, but she did.* She was aware of the unspoken words. She saw the looks being exchanged between people. She needed someone to tell her the truth.

"Mama, please tell me," Annie begged.

Betz looked at Will, engrossed in what he was doing. She gestured to Eugene, showing him that she was taking Annie elsewhere. Betz sat in a chair, pulling Annie down with her, hugging her tight. Betz wanted to tread lightly, yet honesty was more important, particularly with this child.

"Dear, Papa was in a dreadful accident. His legs are damaged. They may mend with time. However, he lost a lot of blood. You know how important blood is to our bodies. He lost more than he should. It's making him really sick."

"Is he going to die?"

"Honey, no one knows for sure."

"I want to see him. Please, Mama."

"Of course. Will and you can both see him."

"Now?"

"Now."

They walked back to where Will was still coloring his picture. Betz sat by him, with Annie by her side.

"Will, dear. Look at me." Will looked up, and stopped what he was doing. "We are going to see Papa now. Please, don't be afraid of the noisy machines around him. He is in a deep sleep. He won't wake up to talk to you, but you can talk to him. Ok?"

"Ok, Mama. Let's go."

Betz grasped both hands. Together, they walked the corridor until they reach Kenneth's room. Annie took the lead, Will following behind. Betz nodded to Evelyn, who quietly slipped out, allowing the family to be alone. Will, intimidated by the machines, stood back. Annie courageously walked to where her Papa laid. She began speaking, telling him all kinds of stories like she did when Will was younger, cooped up in bed.

Will, seeing his sister, walked closer to the bedside. He began talking about the snowy trip to the hospital. He showed him the picture he was coloring for him. Tears silently streamed down Betz's face. Kenneth was so good with the children. They adored him. *How will I manage without him?* Shocked by her thought, she chastised herself. She wasn't giving up hope yet.

Margaret came into the room. "I'm sorry, but I'm required to do my check again."

Betz instructed Will and Annie to say goodbye to their father. She pushed the chair closer to the bed so they could easily reach him. Each child took turns kissing him on the forehead. "Night, Papa," Will said. "See you in the morning."

Betz guided the children back to the lounge area where the others waited. Eugene handed her a much-needed coffee. She took a sip, thankful for the hot liquid. Not wanting to leave Kenneth by himself, she hurried back to her vigil by his side, where she remained the rest of the night. She tried to remain calm and brave, but she broke down and cried. Resting her cheek on his hand, she dozed off until she heard footsteps in the doorway.

Kenneth's parents had arrived. Donald placed his hand on Betz's shoulder. She stood as he engulfed her in his enormous arms. Elizabeth, immediately began crying when she saw her son, looking deathly ill. Betz hugged her, whispering how glad she was they were here.

Donald suggested she take a break, ensuring her they would stay with Kenneth. Reluctantly, she agreed. In the restroom, she splashed water on her face before heading to the lounge area, where Evelyn and the others sat. Annie and Will were curled up in a chair, fast asleep. Evelyn's head was resting on Stuart's shoulder. Eugene had his chin on his chest, snoring. It had been a long night for everyone.

Evelyn sensed her presence first. She raised her head and gently removed Stuart's hands around her waist. He stirred. Evelyn whispered something in his ear before walking to Betz. She put her arm around her shoulder, leading her away. "Let's get you something to eat."

"I'm not hungry," replied Betz.

"Be sensible. You can't let yourself get to a point of exhaustion. Something hot will do you good."

Evelyn was already steering her towards the cafeteria. Betz barely touched the oatmeal Evelyn had chosen for her. She welcomed the hot coffee, though. The two women began talking. Betz confessed she was unsure she had the strength to get through this. Evelyn assured her she did, that she wasn't alone. She had friends who loved her. They would help with whatever she needed.

Betz, eager to get back upstairs, drank the last remnants of her coffee before refilling her cup to take with her. She wished to check on the kids first, though Evelyn assured her they were fine.

"Eugene has been wonderful," Evelyn said. "He's good with the kids."

It reminded Betz to do something nice for him when all this was over.

When they returned upstairs, everyone was awake. Betz was talking to the children when she saw Dr. Mertz coming towards her. Alarm bells went off in her head as she headed in his direction. He waited for her to come to him, away from the children. He had just finished making his rounds, and reviewing Kenneth's charts.

Woefully, he said, "Kenneth is deteriorating further. I ordered his morphine be increased. He appears to be experiencing pain. We don't want that."

Betz nodded, evidence she heard him. She understood what increasing the drug meant. She experienced the same thing with her mother.

"I'm sorry I can't do more. His injuries are too severe," he said as he patted her shoulder before turning and walking away.

Betz could not move, her feet rooted to the floor. Evelyn, seeing her distress came to rescue her. Betz explained what the doctor told her. Together, they decided there was no reason the children should stay any longer. Evelyn and Stuart would take them home.

Saying goodbye to the kids was hard. Betz wanted to cling to them, keep them near her, but knew this wasn't a place for young children.

She sat in a chair next to them and explained. "Auntie Evelyn needs help. Could you please be kind enough and go back home with her?"

Annie began to protest, but she was tired of sitting around doing nothing, so she agreed. Betz wrapped a scarf around her neck, kissing her on the top of her head. "I need you to be a good big sister," Betz told her.

"I will Mama. Tell Papa I love him."

"I will."

Betz did not wait to watch them leave. She hurried back to her husband.

Kenneth's parents refused to leave even when Betz insisted. They watched as Margaret increased the morphine once again.

Betz leaned over and whispered in Kenneth's ear. "It's ok. I will be ok. It's time for no more pain. It's time to go. I love you. I will always love you."

Kenneth took his last breath on that fateful February morning with his wife and parents by his side.

Chapter 25

Kenneth listened, hearing the beep, beep of a machine. A sound he did not recognize. *What was it?* He could not place it. He tried moving, but couldn't. His body frozen. He couldn't feel a thing. *What was wrong?*

He heard movement. Someone was in the room. He heard talking. They were discussing him. Someone stating the extent of his injuries were irreparable. A female voice explaining the massive amount of blood loss before arrival. *Was he injured in the war? Was he in a field hospital?*

Then he recalled Betz. *Betz and I married. I returned from the war. We have children. Don't we?* He questioned himself. *Was it a dream or was he still in Korea?* He became confused, disoriented.

He heard more talking. *Keep his legs wrapped. Check the dressings in an hour. Notify me if there is any immediate change. Has anyone contacted the family? Let me know when they arrive. I'm not sure how this young man survived this horrific accident.*

Were they talking about him? He found it hard to believe. He had no pain. He couldn't feel a thing. He was fine. Wasn't he?

He fell back to sleep. The only sound coming from the machine beeping. He awoke to more talking outside his door. A man talking. *Ma'am, I remind you the next few hours are critical. It will tell us a lot. Prepare yourself.*

Kenneth heard the curtain being pulled back. A heart-wrenching moan that grabbed at his gut. The sound of heels coming closer. A hand to his face, brushing the hair from his forehead. A kiss. Her cheek resting on his own. He felt the wet tears. Words of love pouring from his wife's mouth.

He wanted nothing more than to grab her, return the affection, but he couldn't move. This woman meant the world to him.

Another person entered. *Sorry for the interruption.* A familiar voice. If he had to guess, he'd say it was a nurse. *It's time to check his vitals.* A rustling of blankets. A gasp. A scraping chair.

The nurse introduced herself as Margaret. *The crush injuries to his legs are substantial. We are watching closely for signs of infections. I was here when they brought him in. We stabilized him, but the blood loss was significant. It was touch and go for a couple of hours.*

He heard his wife asking hard, detailed questions. Pride exuded. She knew what she was talking about. Margaret answered the best she could. *Why didn't he recognize how intelligent his wife was?* Her understanding of medical terms was beyond anything he expected. He felt shame. He never appreciated the skills she learned while he was away at war. She was obviously modest. *Why the hell didn't I talk to her more about it?*

The conversation continued. *His skin feels cold and clammy. He's so pale. His pulse is weak. These are not good signs.*

Unfortunately, no, they are not. We'll know more by tomorrow if...

If what? No one finished the sentence.

Quiet again. A hand covering his own. He drifted in and out of sleep. He felt sweaty and chilled.

Voices again. *Look who's come to see you? It's Evelyn.*

Evelyn, he wanted to cry. *Betz will need you more than ever.*

He heard Evelyn talking about nonsensical, everyday tidbits. He was grateful she was here for his wife. He wished he could tell her so.

A few moments later, he heard Annie's melodic voice. She began telling stories about school, the music teacher, and all the wonderful things he loved to hear about. *My dear Annie, I don't tell you enough what a delight you are. You are so creative. Your own person. You will do your own thing. I see it. I know it. Please, be careful. Your free spirt can get you in trouble. I love you.*

Papa? It was Will. He began telling him about the snowy trip here. *I colored a picture just for you. It's you driving your big truck. I hope you like it. I was careful to stay in the lines, just like you told me.*

Kenneth planned to teach this young boy so many things. His son had been through a lot at an early age, but overcame the obstacles. He will grow to be a fine young man. He will take care of his Mama. *I love you, Will. I wish I had been there more for you.*

Margaret again. *I'm sorry, but I need to do my check again.*

Betz. *Say goodbye to your father.* A chair scraping the floor, being moved closer to the bed. He felt the kiss on the forehead from each child. *Night, Papa. See you in the morning.*

No, don't go. He wanted to cry out. There were so many things left unsaid. So many lessons to teach his children. *Be good for your Mama.* Words he always said to them. *Would they remember?*

Asleep again. Drifting in and out. The pain. *When did that start?* He heard muffled crying. *Were those wet tears he felt on his hand?* Then deep breathing. Betz finally asleep. She was still here. He was so tired.

He heard footsteps approaching. He smelled the mixture of his father's soap and aftershave, Dove and Old Spice. Betz stirred. Her cheek no longer resting on his palm. A scuff of a chair moving. His father whispering to Betz. He couldn't understand what he said. His mother, crying. Betz telling his parents how glad she was they came. He felt his mother's lips on his cheek.

Betz, why don't you take a break? We'll stay with him. Get some coffee. Check on the children. His wife protested. His father insisting. The sound of heels. Betz was leaving the room.

He wished he could talk. To tell his parents to take care of his wife and children. The pain was increasing. He winced. His mother fluffed his pillow underneath his head. She worried about everything. He wished she had not come. He did not want to cause her more distress. His father, pacing back and forth, was driving him mad. He drifted into sleep again.

They pulled the covers back. The doctor examining him. He winced. More pain. His father asking his status. *I'm afraid he's worsening. His vitals are slowing. His urine output is minimal. A sign his body is not recovering from the blood loss. I'm concerned about his pain. I will discuss with Mrs. Johnson, but I believe we need to increase his morphine to control the pain.*

Yes, please, doc. I don't want him to feel pain. Do whatever you can.

The doctor's footsteps retreating. His mother praying between her sobs. *Stop pacing.* His father, a man of few words, stopped at the edge of the bed. *I'm proud of you, son. I wished I told you more often. I have always loved you. I hope you know that.*

I know. I love you too, Dad. You too, Mom.

Betz's heels hurrying to his room. The nurse next to his bed. A warm sensation in his body. The pain finally lessened.

Betz leaning over, whispering in his ear. *It's ok. I will be ok. It's time for no more pain. It's time to go. I will always love you.*

That was all it took. He needed her permission to leave. He was so tired.

I love you too, Betz. More than you'll ever know.

Steadily, his mind slowed down. He no longer heard anything. No longer felt pain. No longer breathed.

Chapter 26

Donald placed his hand on her shoulder. "He's gone, Betz. Come."

She stared straight ahead in disbelief. Her feet once again, rooted to the floor. She took one big gulp before forcing herself to move. She let her father-in-law lead her away from her husband's bed. She heard the *clip clop* of her heels on the tiled floor. The sound of Elizabeth next to her sobbing resounded in her ears. She did not weep. She was in shock.

Years later, whenever Betz looked back on that day, she remembered the sounds. They remained acutely vibrant in her head. It was amazing how her brain shut out some things, but let her recall others with utmost clarity.

Donald guided her and Elizabeth to the lounge area. To Betz's surprise, Eugene was still there, half asleep in a chair. She assumed he left with the others. Her father-in-law firmly told her to sit. She did as she was told. He looked at her, hands tightly clasped in her lap. He worried about the lack of response from her.

Sensing others approaching, Eugene lifted his head. The sullen looks on their faces said it all. He suddenly stood, taking Mrs. Johnson by the arm, aiding her to a seat nearby. A clenched handkerchief to her mouth, she could not stop sobbing. His own eyes filled with sorrow, knowing today they lost a great man.

After the women were seated, Kenneth's father beckoned to Eugene. Donald was feeling conflicted. He felt it his duty to drive Betz back to Brimmer, but he had a farm to consider. They left immediately after they received the phone call regarding the accident. There hadn't been time to plan. He felt he had to return home.

He did not want his daughter-in-law making funeral arrangements alone. They'd come to stay for a few days to assist her with that. After discussing it further, it made sense for Eugene to drive Betz back home. He promised he'd remain with her until Evelyn brought the kids back. He was confident Evelyn could stay until the Johnsons arrived in a couple of days.

Eugene sympathized with Donald. His wife was a wreck. He just lost his son. His daughter-in-law had no family to help her. They lived hours apart, so it would not be easy. A lot was riding on his shoulders. He had a lot of responsibility, and you could see fatigue in his eyes already. It was a long trip home for all of them.

Kenneth's parents stood. Donald helped his wife wrap herself in the heavy coat she wore. Eyes still streaming with tears, she clung to Betz.

"My poor dear." She kept saying.

Donald disengaged his wife from the stronghold she held. He grabbed Betz in an enormous bear hug without saying a word. He then steered Elizabeth towards the elevator.

"We'll see you in a couple of days," Donald choked out.

Eugene held Betz's coat as she slipped her arms into the sleeves. She raised her hand, acknowledging she heard Kenneth's father. The door to the elevator opened. Kenneth's parents stepped in. Before the door closed, Eugene witnessed Elizabeth slumping into her husband's arms, grieving.

He turned to Betz, not sure what to say.

"Are you ready?" he kindly asked.

She went to grab for her handbag. It wasn't there. Eugene noticed panic written on her face.

"I left my purse in Kenneth's room," she exclaimed.

Eugene began walking in that direction.

She grabbed his arm. With barely a whisper, said, "Please, let me. I want to say goodbye once more."

Eugene, not knowing what to do, thinking it wasn't a good idea. "Are you sure?" he asked.

"Yes," she said as she began walking down the corridor.

When she reached the room, she hesitated. She pushed open the door, taking a deep breath. She saw her purse on the floor next to the chair she had sat in for hours. Kenneth was still lying in the bed. The machines no longer making their rhythmic sounds. She bent over, retrieving her pocketbook from the floor. She walked over to the bed, touching her husband's face with her palm.

"I thought we had forever. We'd grow old together. You promised me our kids would grow up with a father. They need both of us. I'm not sure I can do this by myself. I don't want to do this. It's not fair. Why did you leave me too?"

She turned and walked away for the last time, completely shattered.

She met Eugene at the elevator. Avoiding his eyes, she looked straight ahead. She didn't say a word as they descended to the lobby floor. He looked at her sideways. He'd experienced nothing like this. He felt awkward and clumsy. Should he stay silent? Should he talk? What should he do? All these thoughts going through his head.

When they reached the lobby doors, Eugene told her to wait there, until he brought the car around. She refused. She said she needed to walk. It was a short distance since he found a close parking spot upon their arrival. The snow had stopped. The sidewalks were shoveled, but still slick. The heels Betz was wearing were not meant for snow. She began to slip. Eugene grabbed her arm, keeping her upright. She then tucked her arm into his until they set foot in the parking lot. He unlocked the passenger door, allowing her to slide into the bench seat. He walked to the driver's side, opening the door. He turned the key in the ignition, leaning forward, cranking the heat to high. The cold blast made Betz shudder.

"It should be warm in a minute," he said as he slammed the door.

Eugene, well prepared for snow in Wisconsin weather, took the brush lying on the floor of the backseat. He began brushing the snow from the car windows. It took effort to remove the heavy white stuff. He was glad for the distraction, trying to prepare himself for the ride home with his friend's widow. His hands were becoming icy and cold. The headlights and taillights were the only things remaining.

He could not postpone getting back into the car any longer. He placed the brush back on the floorboard in the backseat. He stomped his feet before getting into the driver's seat. Warm air was coming from the vents. He took off his wet gloves and blew on his hands before turning to his passenger.

"Betz, I'm so…"

She held her hand up to silence him. "Eugene, please don't say you're sorry. I'm so tired of those words. What does that really mean, anyway? I know, I know. I say it too when someone dies, but the words…" She let the rest of the sentence hang. "I appreciate all you've done for me and the kids. Please know that. I'm just so tired right now. Tired of life."

"I understand. Please know I'm here for you if you want to talk."

"Thanks, Eugene."

Eugene put the car into reverse. He no longer worried about doing the wrong thing. Betz dictated the course of their journey back to Brimmer. She had to determine what that was. Eugene would stay silent, concentrating on the road only.

Betz drifted in and out of sleep. Eugene pondered about the woman next to him. He realized he did not know her well. He met Kenneth a few years back. They both worked at the same company. They occasionally socialized together. He'd been invited to some of the same gatherings as Evelyn and Stuart. Betz was always congenial. His impression of her was that she was always serious, and quiet. He'd seen her friend Evelyn pull her out of her shell, making her laugh, so he knew she had a different side to her, too.

They stopped for gas, using the restroom and buying coffee.

When they got back into the car, Betz asked, "You doing alright driving?"

He responded in the affirmative.

Betz sipped her coffee. Her head against the passenger window. "He abandoned me just like all the others."

"What do you mean?" Eugene asked.

"My father, my mother, Neil, now my husband. They all abandoned me. Left me."

Eugene knew her mother had passed away from cancer. He was not aware of what happened to her father. He had no clue who Neil was.

She kept talking. "My mother died from cancer several years ago. She never knew my children. She never saw me as a mother. Neil, Dr. Miller, was a man I admired. As a child, I dreamed he would become my father. He moved away to a different city. I cried for days. My dreams shattered. My mother never knew how devastated I was when he left. My chance to have a father gone. I couldn't believe he didn't love us enough to take us with. We remained living with my grandmother until she died. My mother bringing me up alone."

Betz took another sip of her coffee. "Neil came back into our lives again. My mother was so happy. I had just met Kenneth. Both of us excited for our futures." She stopped for a moment before continuing. "The police came right before Christmas. The officer stating there had been a car accident. Dr.

Miller, Neil was on his way to our house that snowy night. An engagement ring was found in his car, wrapped and trimmed with a beautiful bow. He was coming to propose to my mother. Her chance to be happy. I was happy. I loved Kenneth. She no longer had to be responsible for me. It was time for her to live. Then he died. She was never the same after that. I swear, the cancer progressed more rapidly because she was heartbroken."

Eugene did not say a word. He let her talk.

"I'm sure you've heard the stories. I don't know my father. I'm illegitimate. It was hard growing up. Kids were cruel. When my mother died, she did not have the courtesy to tell me his identity. I even asked her when she was dying. Nothing. I have nothing. My father abandoned me."

Eugene had been looking straight ahead the whole time she was talking. He looked at her then. She was looking out the window. He wondered if she was even aware of him, aware of who she was speaking to.

She continued. "I've been searching for him, you know. Ever since my mother died. I need to find him. I need to know my story." She became silent. "I have searched the house. I have gone to county records. Nothing. I have found nothing. No one in Brimmer will tell me. My father is nameless. Was it his choice? Or my mother's? I do not know."

A twinge went through Eugene. He didn't know this background. It shocked him.

The words kept coming. "Kenneth and I agreed to have a large family. I did not want a child of mine growing up alone, like me. He agreed. After Will got polio, I couldn't bear the pain of exposing another child to life's cruelties. That child suffered so much. The poor kid. He will live with the aftereffects forever. How could I risk that? Not a risk I wanted to take. Now here I am. My husband just died, leaving me to raise two children on my own. It wasn't the plan."

Still, she rambled. "I'm not like my mother. I don't have the same resilience. I don't have the same capability to overcome that much pain and loss. I never will."

Shocked at Betz's confession, Eugene looked at her differently. He interjected.

"No, you are not your mother. You are Betz. You are your own person. Quiet, kindhearted, loving Betz. You have experienced enough tragedy to last a lifetime. Those tragedies will help you through this. You can do this. You must."

She remained quiet for the rest of the trip. Eugene hoped he did not overstep the boundaries, saying what he did. He probably shouldn't have said anything.

Who was he to give advice? She just lost her husband, for goodness' sake. What was he thinking? What had he just done?

Chapter 27

Betz headed to the kitchen immediately after she unlocked the door and hung up her coat. She made a pot of coffee. *That's what a person does. Isn't it?* Eugene was a guest. She knew he wouldn't leave, even though she wanted him to. She wanted to be alone with her thoughts.

It wasn't long after when Evelyn arrived with the children. They ran into their mother's arms. Wrapping them in a huge embrace, Betz had no words. She simply held them. Will, with a muffled voice, asked. "How's Papa?"

"Dear, please go sit in the living room. I'll be right in. I want to thank Eugene for helping us."

Eugene was already shrugging on his coat.

She stood directly in front of him. "Thank you… for everything. Those words don't suffice for everything you did. I'm truly grateful for driving us in the snow, for watching the children, for bringing me back, for everything." She hugged him, giving him a kiss on the cheek. "Thanks again." She said as she stood back.

Embarrassed, Eugene wasn't sure how to respond. "You're welcome. Please call if there is anything I can help with. I mean that."

He bid goodbye to Evelyn before leaving. Once outside, he exhaled a big breath of air. Exhaustion overcame him. A stiff drink is what he craved, but first he needed sleep.

Evelyn followed Betz into the living room. Together, they'd tell the kids what happened to their father. Evelyn lit the logs in the fireplace while Betz sat between Annie and Will on the velvet sofa.

Annie already knew her Papa was not returning home. Will, with widened eyes, asked about him again. Betz gently told him Papa had too many injuries. There was nothing the doctors could do to help him.

"He died, Will."

As tears streamed down his cheeks, she held him.

"Be brave. Papa would want you to be brave. Can you do that?" Will nodded his head.

Annie walked over to Evelyn, hugging her tight, saying, "I know, darling girl. I know. It'll be ok."

Annie left, soon coming back with two cups of coffee. One she handed to her mother, the other to Evelyn. She grabbed Will's hand, pulling him with her. "Let's go play a game. We'll go to your room." She looked back at the two women, seeing their mouths agape.

Evelyn couldn't help it. She snickered. When she tried to keep it in, she snorted. Betz began laughing hysterically. Evelyn sat next to Betz, holding her stomach. "That girl," she blurted out. Betz couldn't respond, she was gasping for breath.

They looked at each other. The laughter suddenly stopped. Evelyn reached over. Betz fell into her arms, sobbing. "I'm so mad at him," she exclaimed. "I'm just so mad for him to leave me like this."

Evelyn tried to soothe her, surprised by the anger. For the longest time, they sat there. Betz, unable to keep her eyes open any longer, excused herself to get some sleep. Evelyn stayed, ready if her friend needed her.

The next day, Betz received a call from Mr. Bailey to express his sympathies. He told her what an outstanding employee Kenneth was. He informed her that Bailey Oil was overseeing the return of Kenneth's truck. He inquired if he could do more. Betz couldn't think of anything else. He told her to let him know. When she hung up the phone, she remembered she still had little information about the cause of the accident.

The Johnsons arrived two days later. Donald took control. An appointment with The Ferguson Funeral Home was already scheduled. Betz was glad she didn't have to do this alone.

The three of them arrived on time. Once inside, Betz became overwhelmed. She had done this before, but Kenneth was there to help. She contributed little to the decision making, letting her father-in-law choose.

There was a slight disagreement over the burial site, though. Kenneth's parents suggested he be laid to rest in the town he was born in. Betz was adamant he be buried in a plot next to her mother. Betz won.

It was obvious Kenneth's mother was overcome with grief. However, today, she seemed much calmer. When she asked Donald about it, he admitted he asked the doctor prescribe Librium for her.

"She was acting way too high-strung. I couldn't get her to settle down. It wasn't good for her to worry about everything. The drug helps to keep her even-keeled," he said.

The day of the funeral, Betz walked down the aisle, following the casket, a child on each side. Donald and Elizabeth followed directly behind her. Kenneth's siblings, most married by now, came next in line. Betz was ushered into the front pew, where she sat with Annie and Will.

She listened to the sermon; the words making little sense to her. Her thoughts focused on one phrase, 'Everything happens for a reason.' *And what reason would that be?* She'd really like to know. The idea was absurd.

She tried to concentrate on the service, but so many memories filtered through her head, it was hard.

The eulogy given by Kenneth's brother was beautiful.

"Kenneth was a noble son, great brother, great husband, great father,"

Kenneth was all that. She loved him with all her heart. She had to stop being angry at him for leaving her.

Deep snow covered the ground. They traipsed through the cemetery to the gravesite. The pallbearers struggled with the casket, trying to keep from slipping. Betz looked to her right at her mother's tombstone. Barely peeking through the snow were the remnants of the yellow rose. Strange how she noticed it through the snow.

Once the gravesite ceremony was over, the group made their way back to the church basement. A lunch provided by the church's women's group awaited them. Annie and Will saw Evelyn's kids, and ran over to meet them. It would be hard to get the children to eat today. Betz wasn't even going to try.

People slowly began leaving, wishing her well. Eugene saw an opportunity to speak to her. He wanted to make sure she was doing alright. He reiterated that if she needed anything, to let him know. He was there to help. She thanked him once again for all he did.

That evening, she told Donald she wanted to know the details of what happened. He repeated what he was told, and added.

"They found the man in Dubuque. The trucker had no clue his trailer ran over someone's legs. It horrified him to learn what happened. After talking to him, the police declared it was an accident. There were no charges pressed against him."

"Yes, a horrible accident," Betz repeated quietly.

The Johnsons left the next day. They needed to return to the farm. Betz was on her own. In her wildest dreams, she never imagined she'd be in this position. Building a life without Kenneth was going to be difficult.

Chapter 28

Since the day Betz returned from Iowa City, people had surrounded her for days. The house always full, everyone asking what she needed, making sure she was ok. Then nothing. Everyone returned to their lives. Even Annie and Will returned to normalcy, heading back to school. Life was not normal for Betz. Her husband would never walk through their door again. He would never come home to her.

Kenneth's semi was returned to Brimmer. Mr. Bailey called, saying he had someone in mind who may be interested in buying it. He volunteered to help Betz with the sale. She was grateful for his help. It was one less thing to deal with. They invested a lot of money in that truck. She trusted Mr. Bailey to get her the best possible deal. Unfortunately, used trucks were not worth what she hoped. The money received was less than one might expect.

Her inheritance had slowly been dwindling over the past few years. The medical cost for Will's treatment had not been cheap. The frequent trips to the Mayo Clinic and overnight stays put a dent in their savings. There were no regrets. She would have spent every penny she had to help her child. Will's health was worth every cent.

The investment made in Kenneth's truck took another bite out of their savings. With his paycheck each week, they were doing fine financially. Over time, they knew his increased salary would pay for the truck. The realization there would be no more paychecks hit her. She would not worry about it yet. They were alright, for now.

Eugene showed up one evening, unannounced. He explained he was in the neighborhood. He was checking to make sure there was nothing she needed. She invited him in for a drink. It was the least she could do for all he'd done for them. The conversation was easy between them.

Eugene was intrigued by Betz, especially after what she shared with him on their way back to Brimmer. It was a nice evening. Eugene bid her goodnight, saying he'd check on her again soon.

During the day, Betz wandered through the house aimlessly. Her anger slowly subsided. The resentment turned into feelings of self-pity. *Why me?* She wondered. *What did I do to deserve this?* Betz thought about all the rotten things that happened to her since her birth. It triggered something inside her. *Dammit, father. Why didn't you love me enough to find me? To know me?* It always came back to her father.

She became obsessed. Once again, tearing the house apart, trying to find any remnant of him. She remembered Mae telling her the rumor she heard about her father. He might be a man from Lansbury. She located the picture she found years ago in a book on the shelf. She stared at it. She saw a young man in uniform. No relative had his same likeness in any of the family albums. She placed the picture in her pocketbook. She had an idea.

One day after school, Annie, barely able to contain herself, burst into the back door. She was excited to share the news with her mother. She got a solo for the spring concert. She yelled, but there was no answer. Her mother was nowhere to be found. Disappointed, she made Will a snack, wondering where she could be. Her mother had been acting strange lately. It was unlike her to be gone when they arrived home from school, though.

Breathless, Betz ran into the house. The time had gotten away from her. She had gone to Lansbury where the local library kept records of soldiers from the war. She was hopeful she could match her photograph to one they had in their records. Today, she found nothing, but she wasn't giving up. She'd return tomorrow and the day after if she needed to.

At dinner that evening, Annie talked enthusiastically about the solo she had been selected to perform in front of the whole school. Betz told her how proud she was, but her mind was still on the photo. The man in uniform could possibly be her father, and she was desperate to find a name.

After several weeks, traveling to the neighboring town, Betz concluded it was a futile attempt. Without a name, she was getting nowhere. A dead end, once again.

Evelyn worried about her friend. She called often, wishing she lived closer to her. She sensed Betz's despondency, unsure how to deal with it. Summer was approaching. She hoped the warmer weather would help.

The Fourth of July was a hot and humid day. Betz and the kids arrived at Evelyn's. Sounds of laughter and shouting came from the backyard. When they rounded the corner, Will was blasted with a water balloon. His shirt soaking wet, he ran to join in the fun. Betz carried the pineapple-upside-down cake into Evelyn's kitchen, setting it on the counter with the other desserts.

Stuart greeted her, offering her a beer. She accepted, taking a long swig out of the tall bottle, before setting it down. She was thirsty. She saw Evelyn juggling a tray, and hurried off to help her. She offered to carry the empty tray into the house. She was feeling melancholy. It was the first party she'd gone to without Kenneth. She let out a gigantic sigh. This would not be easy.

Eugene came up behind her. She was glad to see him. She didn't know some couples there, so welcomed his friendly face. For the past several months, he'd been helping her around the house, fixing things when needed. Whenever she called, he willingly came. They were becoming fast friends.

Once the sun went down, the kids lit sparklers. They were warned to be careful, to hold them away from their bodies. The circles of light lit up the yard. Betz noticed Annie standing a little away from the others. Apparently, she was too grown up for sparklers.

When did Annie get this old?

Summer was soon over. The kids returned to school. Betz was unsure what to do with herself throughout the day. It left too much time to think. She became depressed. Life was not going as planned, and she was on the brink of feeling hopeless.

Chapter 29

It was Friday. Betz promised the children they'd play board games and eat popcorn tonight. Feeling slightly guilty for her recent lack of attention, she wanted to make it up to them.

It was late morning when she headed to the grocery store. Her plan was to surprise them with a few other goodies, wanting the night to be memorable. The parking lot was unusually full. She found a cart left near where she parked. She placed her purse on the cart's top and pushed it into the store. In the baking aisle, she selected bark chocolate to make a cake, one of the kid's favorites.

Many of the customers she knew. They kindly asked after her wellbeing. It took her longer than expected to complete her shopping. She stood in the checkout when mayhem erupted.

Mr. Driscoll heard the news over the radio. He ran out from behind the swinging doors, yelling. "The President's been shot. Someone shot the President."

Women all around began sobbing. Betz, in disbelief thought, *who would do such a thing?*

"What is this world coming to?" Someone else shouted.

"I'm sure it's nonfatal. There are wonderful doctors in Dallas." Doris, the cashier said.

Edna Gleason began praying right in the middle of the canned vegetable aisle.

Betz paid the bill for her groceries as quickly as possible. She rushed home and turned on the television set. The cameras depicting tons of people standing outside Parkland Memorial Hospital, waiting for an update.

Then the dreadful announcement. They pronounced President John Fitzgerald Kennedy dead at around 1:30 p.m. Betz quickly walked to the television and changed the channel. Every station was broadcasting the same thing. Chet Huntley talking on one station, Walter Cronkite confirming it on another.

Kenneth and Betz both voted for him. He signified hope for the future. They loved his charismatic smile, Jackie, and the children, too. How he handled the Cuban Missile Crisis was admirable. He prevented a nuclear war.

Grief overcame Betz. The President's death triggered something inside her, leaving her feeling more hopeless. No one was safe. Life was filled with uncertainty. The world was full of sorrow. She felt empty, useless. The depression she'd experienced was taking hold again, more strongly. She felt herself slipping, not able to control it.

Annie and Will came home from school early that fateful November day. The principal made the announcement over the loudspeaker stating President Kennedy was just assassinated. Annie's teacher turned her back from the children. It became clear she was crying. Some of the other kids in her classroom began sobbing, too. The principal stated school would be dismissed shortly. They should go home to be with their families. It was a tragic day.

Will, outside at recess, bundled up from the cold, suddenly heard the bell ring. They were ushered back into the school. One teacher met them at the door, telling them to leave their coats and hats on. Not sure what was happening, the kids sat at their desks with their heavy winter coats on. Mrs. Noble explained they were being dismissed soon. Something tragic happened to President Kennedy. They were being sent home.

Will, the astute student he was, understood the severity of the situation. Other kids in his class did not quite get it, not understanding why the grownups were upset.

When Annie and Will got home, they found their mother sitting in front of the television set. They sat and joined her. Will asked lots of questions. Betz took the time to explain the best she could. "He was a great man," she said with a heavy heart.

For the next three days, the family watched the events unfold. The coverage on TV was extensive. Glued to the television on Sunday, Betz and the children watched the procession down Pennsylvania Avenue. Seven white horses pulled the cart carrying the casket of the former President. The same cart used to carry Franklin D. Roosevelt and the Unknown soldier. A riderless horse followed. The First Lady, walking in between the President's brothers, Robert and Teddy, followed directly behind. The scene in front of them was moving.

The formality enthralled Will. The military presence, the bagpipes playing, the horse-drawn carriage, the succession of people walking behind. His questions continued. Some Betz could answer, others she could not.

Seeing Jackie in her black veil reminded Betz of her own loss. Mesmerized by the commentary, she didn't budge from the sofa. She wanted to disappear to her bedroom, to be alone with her emotions. A tug of war played within herself. The children needed her. Their needs were more important than hers right now.

For weeks, no one talked about anything else. They knew exactly where they were, exactly what they were doing when they heard the news. Everyone tuned into the news coverage. For those few days, in November 1963, the world stood still.

Events after Kennedy's shooting made Betz realize she was in a terrible place. She was not herself. Articles written about the funeral and Jacqueline Kennedy became her obsession. Mrs. Kennedy exuded strength, willpower, and stamina after her husband's assassination. An assassination that occurred right in front of her.

Jacqueline Kennedy reminded Betz of her own mother; a strong, willful, independent woman, able to overcome obstacles. For the last several months, she had not handled Kenneth's death well. Feeling sorry for herself was not becoming. Her children deserved better. She deserved better. It was time to stop wallowing.

After Kenneth left for the military, she was alone, on her own. She found something that made her feel good about herself. She gained self-worth and confidence when she learned the skills of a nursing assistant. She had overcome her own obstacles; being pregnant, having a miscarriage, and raising a child on her own. She did it then. She could do it again.

It was time to make changes. Her head reeling with the thought.

Annie dreaded going home after school. Her mother was always so sad. It was difficult being the older sister, looking after her brother. It was hard to keep Will out of her mother's way. His inquisitive mind always asking questions. The two siblings learned to do things themselves. Will didn't seem to mind, his nose always in one of his books, but Annie missed her mother's companionship. She used to sit and tell her everything, but not anymore. Her mother was always distracted, as if she was living in her own world.

When the children arrived home from school, Annie reminded Will to take off his boots and hang up his coat as they entered the house. Today, their mother was there to greet them at the door. It was like the old days before Papa died. Pleased, Annie smiled brightly. Hot cocoa was waiting for them in the kitchen. Whatever was happening, Annie couldn't be happier. She sensed a change in her mother. She wasn't pretending to be interested in them, like she sometimes did. The atmosphere was noticeably different.

Betz waited until the weekend to discuss her plans with the children. Saturday morning, she made pancakes for breakfast. Annie and Will sat at the kitchen table, talking. Mesmerized, they watched their mother flip a pancake over, making it golden brown on both sides. She seemed happier.

"I have something to share with you," Betz began speaking. "I have not been myself lately. I am terribly sorry about that. It's just that I miss your father so much. I know you do too. I realize I was not being fair to you. It's time we make some changes."

Betz handed a plate of pancakes to Annie.

"Remember how I told you stories about me working at the hospital before you were born? Well, I want to do that again. I need your help, though. I may not always be here when you arrive home from school. Annie, you're old enough now. I trust you to watch over your brother until my shift is over. Do you think you can do that?"

"Yes, mother, I can."

"Will, I know you will be on your best behavior for your sister."

"Yes, Mama, I will."

"Thank you. I don't know what I'd do without you two. I love you so much. I'm so sorry for not being myself."

Later, Betz took Annie aside. "Dear, I know this is a lot of responsibility. I'm confident you can handle it. It's only a short time after school. Please understand I'm not doing this for myself. I'm doing it for us."

Annie understood completely. She'd do whatever it took to rid this house of its sadness and to have her mother back.

The hospital welcomed Betz's application. The need for nursing staff remained. Her prior education, though some time ago, was an advantage. A quick learner, it did not take long for Betz to refresh her skills. Though medicine changed, the care for patients remained the same. Some staff she worked with before, some had retired, others were new. As before, Betz found the work rewarding. It made her a better person, helping others.

The children noticed the difference, especially Annie. Her mother was taking time to be with them, talk with them, do things with them again. The mother they knew and loved was back.

Betz tried to make it up to the children. She knew she got lost for those few months after Kenneth died, but she managed to find her way back.

Chapter 30

Eugene Riley couldn't get the words Betz spoke out of his mind. The things she said on the trip back from Iowa City resonated with him. He couldn't imagine how she overcame what she had. He had not been aware of any of it. Kenneth had never said a word about it. He couldn't relate. His upbringing had been the opposite. He had two loving parents still living, and lots of siblings with nieces and nephews aplenty. When she spoke about the difficulties of being illegitimate, he realized the stigma associated with it. It was obvious it caused undue pain for her growing up. It didn't seem fair she now lost her husband too.

Kenneth was a great guy. They met when he began working at Bailey Oil Company. Kenneth made Eugene feel welcome when he started working there. He invited him to get-togethers at their house. He appreciated it since he was still single. He met Evelyn and Stuart, Betz's good friends, at one of the outings. They all became good friends, especially the guys. Eugene knew how much Kenneth loved his wife.

When Mr. Bailey asked him to take Betz and the children to Iowa City after the accident, he readily agreed. Kenneth was a good friend. He hadn't known how serious his injuries were or that he would be bringing his widow back home.

He remembered thinking how Betz was always so put together. She appeared to be a strong woman, yet quiet. He heard stories about her single mother experience while Kenneth was in South Korea. She exuded confidence, the kind he saw in his own mother.

When he stopped by to check on her after the funeral, he enjoyed talking to her. She was now calling him when she needed something fixed in the house. He was more than happy to comply. He noticed a difference in her, though. She no longer laughed at his jokes. She only snickered politely. It was obvious she was depressed. Who could blame her?

She seemed happy to see him at the Fourth of July party. They spent the afternoon talking, drinking, and having a good time. The children, used to him coming around the house, also acknowledged him. Will was thrilled when he played catch with him in the backyard. It had been a wonderful day.

Eugene did not want to admit he was attracted to Betz, maybe he was more intrigued by her. She was a complex woman. He wished to know her better, but felt guilty. She was his friend's widow.

One night, after a couple of beers, he talked to Stuart about it. Stuart thought it a bad idea. He told him Evelyn was worried about her. Betz was depressed. His wife wasn't sure what to do about it. "She's definitely not ready for a relationship," Stuart said.

Eugene agreed. He'd continue to check on her whenever he could. He wouldn't stop caring about her. After all, they were friends.

Over the next year, Eugene did exactly that. He stopped by, making sure the family was doing fine. He did odd jobs around the house for her; cleaning leaves out of the gutters, helping her rake the lawn, put screens on the windows in springtime, winterize the house in the fall. Many times, Betz asked him to stay for dinner, telling him it was the least she could do. He always agreed. He enjoyed her company and thought she felt the same. His fondness for her continued to grow. He was waiting for the right moment to tell her his feelings. He wanted to be more than friends, but he was content to spend time with her.

One afternoon, they gathered at Evelyn and Stuart's house along with a few other couples. Eugene heard the women talking in the kitchen. Evelyn was trying to convince Betz to attend their class reunion. Betz refused. She said it would be awkward to go as a single person. Evelyn gave her all the reasons she was being silly.

"Come on, Betz. Aren't you curious? Don't you want to see how Phyllis Harvey has aged?" she asked. Phyllis had moved away from Brimmer. She had been one of the popular girls in school, always put together. Her hair always so perfect. "Besides, you need to get out."

"I get out. I come to Lansbury and see you often," Betz retorted back.

"That's not the same thing, and you know it."

Eugene took Betz aside. "If you don't want to go alone to the class reunion, I will accompany you," he volunteered.

A little flustered by his suggestion, she turned slightly away. "No, thank you Eugene. If I decide to go, I'll be fine going alone." She started to head back to the kitchen. "I'm going to see if Evelyn needs any help." Betz was shocked Eugene would consider doing such a thing. *Everyone will think we're a couple if he went with me. What is he thinking?*

In the end, Evelyn convinced Betz to go. Once the decision was made, apprehension turned to excitement. She hadn't attended a class reunion in years. She was actually looking forward to it.

Chapter 31

Betz dressed with more care than usual the night of the reunion. She wasn't sure why. It wasn't like she took great strides with her appearance. Her mother was always dressed smartly, and Betz never understood the importance.

Evelyn advised on what outfit to wear. It was the sixties, styles had changed. Annie kept trying to tell her she needed to get more with the times. Tonight, she took her advice.

Stuart and Evelyn honked the horn. They were right on time. Part of the agreement when she yielded to go was, they'd pick her up, so she didn't have to walk into the reunion by herself. Evelyn was giddy. Stuart was laughing at his wife. Betz was trying her best not to fidget. She wasn't sure why she was nervous.

When they arrived at The Stardust, she noticed the number of cars in the parking lot. Several people could be seen walking into the supper club. At the door stood a table with nametags. Betz found hers first. She was amused when she saw her high school picture above her printed name. *Wow! I have changed.* She didn't realize how much until now. Evelyn grabbed her hand as they made their way around the room. Evelyn, outgoing as always, talked nonstop. Stuart left the women to find a drink. He'd hang at the bar while the ladies gabbed with their old classmates.

Betz was enjoying herself. She talked to classmates she never got to know in school. It was great seeing people in a different atmosphere, in a different phase of life. After a while, she excused herself to use the restroom. She glanced at herself in the mirror. Thinking about her classmates, she realized she was different, too. Life's experiences certainly changed a person.

He saw her first, walking towards the middle of the room. He'd recognize her anywhere. The way she walked, the way she held her head. He continued talking to Ricky, a fellow member of the basketball team, but followed her with his eyes. He noticed she sauntered over to Evelyn who was entertaining a group with a story. Betz smiled at her friend's antics.

Betz looked up. Their eyes met. *Billy, Oh My God, that's Billy!* She saw him walking towards her. She met him halfway.

"It's so nice to see you, Betty," he said.

"Billy, I didn't know you'd be here. I thought you lived in Chicago."

"I did. I just moved back here. My mom is not doing well."

"I'm so sorry to hear that."

"Would you like to sit? Get caught up?" he asked hopefully.

"I'd love to. These shoes are killing my feet." Betz laughed as he pulled out a chair for her to sit down.

"I want to know everything. What have you been doing since you left for college?" Billy asked as he sat down next to her.

Betz sheepishly began speaking. She had broken up with Billy right before leaving for college. She knew she hurt him. When Billy professed his love to her, she told him she wanted to keep her options open. They were too young. They were going in separate directions. Then, a year later, she met Kenneth and fell in love. She heard Billy moved away.

Billy volunteered how devastated he was when she broke up with him. He wanted a fresh start, so his uncle in Chicago found him a job for a glass company. He started out on the production line, and worked hard to prove himself. He'd been promoted several times throughout the years, the last being a production manager, overseeing all the foremen. He enjoyed living in the big city. He liked what it offered.

His Mom became ill about a year ago. It was becoming difficult for his dad to care for her. His father was not in the best health himself. Since he had no personal ties to Chicago - no wife, no kids - he made the tough decision to leave his job and return to Brimmer to help. He just returned this past week. He was still in flux, not having completely moved out of his apartment in Chicago yet.

Several people stopped by their table to say hello throughout the night. She was surprised when Stuart sought her out, telling her it was time to leave. The time spent catching up with Billy flew by. They agreed to meet sometime soon for lunch. He promised he'd call her.

Billy called the following week to tell her he was closing his place in Chicago and completing his move to Brimmer. He really enjoyed seeing her and hoped they could get together once he was settled. It shouldn't take him long to make the move.

Betz wished him luck. She looked forward to seeing him again for old-time's sake. The time spent together at the reunion brought up old feelings. She wondered if it did for him, too.

Chapter 32

Eugene planned to join the family for Sunday dinner the day after the reunion. Betz had extended the invitation the week before. He had been helping her out so much lately, she wanted to show her gratitude. Since Kenneth's death, Eugene became a dear friend. He helped out whenever she needed it, dropping everything else.

Eugene arrived on time. He joked with Annie and teased Will. They got along tremendously with him and always enjoyed their banter. After dinner, Eugene offered to help clear the table. Betz declined. She told him she'd join him for an after-dinner drink in the living room once she and Annie finished in the kitchen.

Eugene poured them each a sherry, waiting for her to join him. He always enjoyed the evenings he spent with Betz and the children. He no longer denied his feelings for her. They'd spent so much time together over the years, and felt their relationship had steadily grown. He was ready to tell her how he felt, but the opportunity never seemed to present itself.

Betz's face was flushed from the heat of the kitchen and doing dishes. Eugene thought she looked beautiful. She accepted the drink he handed her and sat down next to him. She excitedly told him about the class reunion the night before. How much she enjoyed it, and all the people she saw. She mentioned her old flame, Billy, from high school. How they spent the evening catching up.

Something inside Eugene beckoned to him. He cleared his throat.

"Betz, there is something I've been wanting to tell you. I've been waiting a long time." He hesitated before continuing. "I care for you and the kids deeply. I would do anything for you."

"I know Eugene. We care about you too. You have been a rock for me. You've been here whenever I needed anything. I am so grateful. I don't know what I would have done without you."

He took her drink from her, setting both glasses down on the coffee table. He took hold of her hands and looked into her eyes. "Betz, I love you."

Betz, unaware of what was happening, said, "We love you too, Eugene."

"No, Betz. You don't understand. I LOVE YOU!"

She smiled. With a nervous laugh said, "Oh, Eugene. You can't."

When she looked at him, she realized he was serious. She grabbed him in a hug, holding him close. She couldn't bear seeing his sincere face when she whispered. "Eugene, you mean the world to me. I'm sorry. I don't love you… like that."

He stiffened, feeling the heat rising. His face turning red in embarrassment.

She pulled back and touched his cheek. "Eugene, I hold you close to my heart. You have been nothing but gracious and giving. I love you. I do. But I love you as a friend."

He leaped to his feet. "Of course. I'm not sure what I was thinking. It must have been the alcohol talking. I'm sorry I said anything."

"Eugene, please. Sit down. Let's talk."

"There's nothing to talk about. It's fine. I think I better go."

"Eugene…" He was out the door before she could stop him.

I think I just lost a good friend. She thought to herself as she picked up her glass and drank the fiery liquid in one gulp.

Chapter 33

Balancing life between home and work became challenging. Betz loved working at the hospital even though some days it was exhausting. The medical staff continued to appreciate her knowledge. The patients, her compassion. Her feet ached from being on them all day. Her face sometimes froze in a smile, trying to keep spirits high all day. Nobody wanted to stay in the hospital. She did her best to ease their worries, making them feel as comfortable as possible.

The challenges at home were different. The children were old enough now, she no longer worried about leaving them alone anymore. A parent's job is to raise their child to be independent, to make wise choices of their own. Annie, much to Betz's chagrin, made it known she was now a teenager. She was grown up. Nobody could tell her what to do. Therefore, arguments ensued.

Billy often became her sounding board. Since his return to Brimmer, they talked every day. Billy had never married. He confessed he was heartbroken when they broke up. He dated women in Chicago, but they were different. He became engaged once many years ago, but broke it off when he realized her family didn't think he was good enough for her. Since then, he had no serious relationships.

Betz wasn't sure how to feel. She really liked Billy. She always had. She broke up with him, thinking he'd hold her back when she went to college. He moved to Chicago shortly after. How ironic, she ended back in Brimmer, the one place she tried to escape from years ago, and it was Billy who moved to the city. A person never knew where life led.

She welcomed the long conversations on the phone. She no longer dwelled on the past, and its sorrows. The calls eventually evolved into dinner, sometimes a movie. Evelyn jokingly told her they were courting. Betz didn't mind. She rather liked the idea.

One night, not long after the reunion, Billy asked her why everyone called her Betz instead of Betty. She explained it started after she met Kenneth.

"It was his nickname for me. When my mother died, I felt lost. I was beginning a new life. Betz was a name not associated with my mother. It didn't take long for the nickname to stick. Soon, everyone was calling me Betz." Billy became no different.

Billy knew the story of her father, or rather lack of a father, already. Betz told him how obsessed she'd become looking for him. Still, she found no answers. He volunteered to help her. She expressed her frustration, telling him it was useless. He tried to convince her not to give up.

"You never know. Look at us. I showed up in your life unexpectedly," he said.

Betz shared the story of the single yellow rose left on her mother's grave each year on her birthday.

"It's rather bizarre, don't you think? I romanticize it's from my father, and that he loved my mother. Crazy, right?"

"That's not crazy. And yes, it is quite bizarre that someone unknown would do that."

Billy invited Betz to visit his mother. He expressed his concerns about her deteriorating health and knew his mother would love to see her. Betz enjoyed the afternoon, reminiscing about the old days. Billy was right. His mother was failing. She could see the signs immediately.

Both Billy and Betz had their hands full. Billy with his mother, and Betz with Annie.

Tight flared jeans were popular. Annie convinced her mother it was the style everyone was wearing, and she needed a pair. Betz complied and took her shopping. She didn't like how tight they fit, showing off Annie's curves, but bought them anyway. When Annie walked out from her bedroom one day wearing a miniskirt with matching go-go boots, Betz nearly had a heart attack. Words were exchanged.

"Where did you get that outfit?" Betz said rather loudly.

In a defiant voice, Annie said, "I borrowed it from Angie."

"Young lady, you are not old enough to wear a skirt that short."

"Yes, I am, Mother. All the girls are wearing them. I will not change." As she twirled in a circle, Annie said, "I look great."

Betz threw up her hands. As usual, Annie got her way.

The Beatles were dominating the charts. Annie wanted to buy every new 45 record she could get her hands on. She purchased a new transistor radio using her birthday money. Her favorite radio station, WLS Chicago, could be heard throughout the house. Another argument ensued when Annie cranked up the volume as loud as possible when Johnny Lujack came on the air. He played the most current rock and roll hits with Annie singing right along with him. Betz was constantly yelling at her to turn the radio down, Annie ignoring her request.

Billy laughed when Betz told him about Annie's rebelliousness. "We all went through that stage, don't you remember? She's a good kid. She's just testing you." He said in his soothing voice.

Betz didn't think it was funny. She didn't remember being this way as a teenager. She always got along with her mother. Betz thought about the relationship she had with Anneliese. She realized she always tried to please her, always be the good daughter.

Billy's mother passed in early December peacefully in her sleep. It was the old proverb. "She's in a better place."

Betz understood completely. It was still hard to lose a parent, no matter how old they are or how sick they become. She listened to Billy when he needed to talk. She consoled him when he needed a hug. No one understood loss better than she did. At work, she saw families grieving for their loved ones every day. She came to realize no one grieved the same way. Being there for someone was more important. Betz was there for Billy.

Evelyn and Stuart hosted a Packers party on New Year's Eve. They were playing the Cowboys for the NFL Championship. Betz, unsure if they should go, asked Billy anyway. He readily accepted. When they arrived, the men were already tipping back beers; the television tuned into NBC.

Dick Enberg and Merlin Olsen, the announcers for the game gave the weather report. It was -13 with a wind chill of -40. The conditions did not prevent Packers fans from attending. The seats were filled with 50,000 people. The camera panned the crowd, their eyes the only thing showing, the rest of their body covered to protect them from the elements.

The men were glued to the television. The announcers were commenting about the ice on the field. The players were slipping and sliding everywhere. The halftime show was canceled. The marching band's instruments could not be played. The camera showed one of the officials placing a handkerchief on his lips. His metal whistle ripped his skin when he tried to blow it. It was that cold.

The women sat in the corner, talking, when Stuart jumped up from the sofa. "Did you see that?" He yelled. "I don't believe it!" It was the first play of the fourth quarter. The Cowboys just scored, taking the lead. The score 17-14.

"What a pass!" Billy jumped up himself. Dan Reeves threw a halfback option pass fifty yards to Lance Rentzel in the end zone. The Packers now losing by three points.

The women joined the men to watch the rest of the game. Stuart got up and began pacing the floor. The

Packers had the ball with only minutes left in the game.

"I can't watch this," he said.

The women burst out laughing. The clock was ticking down, seconds left on the clock. Bart Starr ran the football in for a touchdown on a quarterback sneak. The men hollered, grabbing their wives, jumping up and down.

"We're going to the World Championship! That was a helluva game."

They had just watched the infamous Ice Bowl.

When they arrived back in Brimmer, Betz made each of them a drink. Sitting in front of the fireplace, they sat holding hands, waiting to ring out the old year and ring in 1968. Billy continued, holding her hand as he bent on one knee. He was holding an open square box in his hand. Against the black velvet lay a beautiful ruby ring. His grandmother's ring.

"Betty Ann. I love you. I've always loved you. I don't want to live another year without you. Will you please do me the honors of becoming my wife?"

Betz, in total disbelief grabbed him, and cried out. "Yes, yes, I will marry you."

"I'm the luckiest man alive." He said as he kissed her full on the lips.

"No, Billy. I'm the lucky one. You came back into my life. I couldn't be happier."

Chapter 34

Betz laid on her bed, hand in the air, staring at the ruby ring on her finger. She couldn't believe she became engaged again in her forties. Her thoughts wandered. She wasn't sure what type of wedding she wanted. She'd been married by the Justice of the Peace before. She was older now. She knew it was practical they do the same. But there was something nagging at her. Billy had never married. She didn't know what he expected. Plus, there was a part of her that wished for a small church wedding. It was something they needed to talk about.

With Annie staying at a friend's house, and Will at his grandparents, they had spent the rest of the wee hours of the early morning in each other's arms. Laying in front of the Christmas tree, a fire blazing in the fireplace, counting their blessings to be given a second chance.

Billy planned on coming for dinner that evening. Will was due home by then and Annie would be back from her overnight. They'd tell the children then.

When Betz got out of bed, she was bursting at the seams. She picked up the phone and dialed Evelyn's number. She had to tell someone the news. The words were barely out of her mouth when she heard a loud squeal. Evelyn could not contain her excitement. She could hear Stuart in the background.

"I knew it. I knew it. Isn't love strange?" Evelyn, not holding anything back said. "Give me the details."

Betz, ecstatic to share, described the proposal to the fullest. She left out the intimate details of the evening. When they finally said goodbye, Betz couldn't stop smiling.

Will arrived first, happy to be home. He wasn't the most comfortable staying at other people's houses, even his grandparents. He hugged his Mama before grabbing a book and heading to his bedroom. As a child, that's where he spent his time. As a teen, it was his happy place.

Betz headed to the kitchen to begin dinner, when the phone rang. It was Billy.

"Betz, it's me."

"Billy, what's wrong? What's all that noise?"

"I'm at the hospital. It's father. They say he's had a stroke."

"Oh no. What happened?"

"He tried taking the Christmas lights down without waiting for me. He collapsed."

"I'll be right there."

"No, Betz. It's New Year's Day. There's nothing you can do here. Spend the day with the kids."

"Billy, I love you. Call me if you need anything. Promise me."

"I love you too. I will."

Annie walked in the front door. She wondered who her mother was talking to. She could hear something in her voice that something was wrong.

"Mother, what's wrong?"

"Billy's father had a stroke."

"That sucks. It's New Year's Day."

"Young lady, where do you come up with such words?"

"Mama, don't start, please."

"I'm going to start dinner." Betz was not in the mood to argue with her daughter.

Annie went upstairs. Carefully placing the record needle down on her new 45, "Daydream Believer." She sat on her bed, knees up, singing to the Monkees. Betz shook her head, listening. Her daughter loved her music as much as Will loved his books.

Betz poured herself a glass of wine. The day wasn't going as planned. She baked the traditional ham, scalloped potatoes and green beans, the menu for New Year's Day for the past several years. She stood at the bottom of the stairs and called to the kids.

"Dinner's almost ready. Please come set the table."

Both kids sauntered into the dining room, Annie grabbing plates and silverware, Will grabbing the water glasses and napkins. They placed them on the table as they'd been taught. Betz brought in the dishes filled with food, setting them in the center of the table. The three sat in their designated chairs. After saying grace, they took turns filling their plates with the delicious food.

Betz passed Annie the platter of ham. Annie gasped. Betz looked at her. Annie's mouth was wide open.

"Whatever is the matter with you?" Betz asked.

In an outraged voice, Annie yelled. "What's on your finger?"

Betz self-consciously covered her ring with her other hand. With all the excitement, she forgot to take it off. She planned to remove it until Billy and she talked to the kids together. It was too late.

"We'll talk after dinner."

"I'm not hungry." Annie informed her as she pushed her plate back.

"Annie, for goodness' sake." Betz took a deep breath. "Ok then. Billy proposed last night. I have accepted his proposal. We are going to be married. We wanted to tell you together." She looked at her children. "Please, be happy for me," she pleaded.

Annie felt tears brimming her eyes. It wasn't that she didn't like Billy. She did. She didn't like change, and no one could ever replace Papa.

Will, being the practical son he was, asked questions. "When? Where? What happens next?"

Betz had no answers at the moment. This was new to her, too. They still had things to discuss. "I value your input. I will respect your opinions. I want to remind you, though. You will attend college in a couple of years. Your life will move on. This is my future. He makes me happy."

Will, gallantly stood up and hugged her. "Mama, if he makes you happy, I'm happy."

Annie sat silent. Her emotions were a roller coaster. She knew she should be happy for her mother. She found it impossible to say the words. Instead, she kissed her on the cheek and retreated to her bedroom.

Will helped Betz clear the table. "Don't worry. She'll come around," he said.

"I hope so. I know it may be shocking to you, but I've known Billy a long time. He's a good man."

"I know he is." He said with assurance.

When Billy called later to give her an update, she told him what transpired.

"I'm sorry you handled that by yourself. I'll make it up to you and to them," he promised.

Betz had the next couple of days off. She promised to come to the hospital in the morning to check on them. When she hung up the phone, she sat in front of the fireplace, feeling guilty. *Did she not deserve to be happy?*

Confident Kenneth would not have wanted her to spend her years alone, she pleaded. *Please, let me know I'm making the right decision.*

That night she dreamed she was in a white, flowing dress. She was a bride, getting ready to walk down the aisle. She was beaming. She slipped her arm under a man's. At last, she found her father. When she turned to look at him, it was Kenneth's face she saw, smiling down on her.

She awoke with a start.

Any doubts about her decision to marry Billy, disappeared. Kenneth approved.

Chapter 35

Betz drove to the hospital the next day. The doctor determined Harold, Billy's father, had a stroke. It occurred on the left side of his brain, leaving his body paralyzed on the right. He was awake. His face had an obvious droop. He had aphasia and was unable to communicate. The medical staff was unsure if he'd ever talk again. Often, speech improved with time, but the severity of his stroke and his age made it unlikely.

The nurse in Betz took over. She couldn't help herself. She immediately looked at the numbers on the monitor. He was currently stable. A good sign. She held a glass of water with a straw, trying to get him to drink. It was obvious he was having difficulty swallowing. She fluffed his pillows behind his head to make him more comfortable. She then tucked the blanket in around him on both sides. He tried to thank her, but his mouth wouldn't work. She took a cloth, swiping the tears she saw in his eyes. She told him it was ok. She understood.

Betz worked with stroke patients before. She knew it would be difficult for Harold to recover fully from this. He just lost his wife a short time ago, and now this.

Billy's sisters arrived, traveling hours to get there. Betz took the opportunity to grab a coffee from the cafeteria, leaving the family to console each other. Betz knew Billy's sisters, but not well. They were older than Billy and her. They had already left home when the two began dating. She'd seen them during the summers and holidays, but spent limited time with them.

Billy found Betz sitting, looking out into space. He hugged her before taking a seat in the opposite chair. She held his hands in hers.

"Betz, tell me the truth. How bad is it?" he asked with sadness in his eyes.

Unsure how blunt she should be, she carefully explained. "Age is not on his side. He wasn't in the greatest health before this happened. He appears to be stable, which is a good sign. His paralysis is a concern. It's possible he could regain some movement, but if I had to bet, it is unlikely. I'm sorry, Billy. The doctor can tell you more. Don't go by what I say."

"If he can't walk, how is he going to go home? If he can't swallow, how am I to care for him?"

"The doctor will discuss all the options. Billy, he survived. He's alive."

"It's not how he'd want to live." Billy buried his head in his hands.

"We'll get through this. We'll manage."

"Thanks for being here, Betz." He looked up under his lashes. "Have I told you lately how much I love you?"

She laughed. "Yes, you have. Now go back to your family. Call me later," she said.

He promised he would.

Harold remained in the hospital for the next two weeks. He was being discharged and admitted to the neighboring nursing home. There was no other choice. He couldn't go home. He needed more care than the family could give him. The nursing home was in the country, halfway between Brimmer and Lansbury. It had a good reputation. It is where he'd get the best care.

Betz went with Billy the day he was admitted to the long care facility. It took them both, along with staff from the hospital, to maneuver him into the passenger seat. Harold, exhausted from the effort, looked defeated. Betz patted him on the shoulder from the backseat. She felt sorry for him. She couldn't imagine what he must be thinking. The need to rely on others for his basic activities had to be hard for him.

Billy drove the short distance to Oakwood Hills. As its name implies, oak trees flanked both sides of the driveway, leading up to the front door. A beautiful setting for a nursing facility.

They managed to help Harold out of the car, into the wheelchair without complication. Billy pushed his father through the double doors to admissions. They were expecting them. The hospital already sent over Harold's medical history, including his post-stroke symptoms. He hadn't recovered his right-side mobility in the last two weeks. It was difficult to understand him, his aphasia still prominent. His swallowing somewhat improved, but he was limited to eating liquid foods.

After the paperwork was completed, they headed towards his assigned room, 5A. His roommate was someone they knew. Billy greeted him like an old friend. Harold ignored him, not seeming to care. It was obvious he didn't want to be there. He pointed to his bed. Billy and Betz exchanged looks. Depression was common amongst stroke patients, and Harold was certainly displaying signs of it.

Betz was leaning forward, saying something to Harold, her back towards the door. A familiar voice greeted them. When Betz turned, she let out a cry of recognition. "Marj," she cried out. She ran and threw her arms around the nurse who just walked in.

"Betz. Is that you?" she asked.

Billy looked back and forth between the women, not sure what was happening.

Betz stepped back. "Billy, this is my good friend Marj, whom I haven't seen in years. She was in the same nursing assistant class as me. By the looks of her nametag, she is now an RN. Marj, this is my fiancé, Billy."

Marj stepped forward and shook Billy's hand. The professional she was, she looked at Harold, not wanting to ignore her patient. "And who is this young fella?"

"That's Billy's father, Harold." Betz volunteered.

"Well, it looks like he wishes to lie down. Let's get him settled first. Then we'll talk."

Marj took over, helping Harold into bed. Billy unpacked his father's small suitcase, placing items within his reach. He packed lightly, not sure what his father may want or need. He'd bring more later.

Content her patient had everything he needed, the three left the room as Harold began to doze off. Marj led them to a small family room at the end of the hallway. Betz wanted to ask so many questions, but knew Marj was working. Now was not the time to renew their friendship.

"I know you can't talk now. I've missed you. I can't wait to catch up. Let's get together soon," Betz said.

"My schedule is crazy right now. We're short-handed. I'll call you to set up a time to meet. It's been too long." Marj often wondered where life led Betz. They got along splendidly during their time together at the hospital. It was too bad they lost touch. She had considered her a good friend back then.

Billy watched Marj tuck a piece of hair behind her ear as she talked. Uncanny, Betz had the same habit. Betz's elated reaction to someone she hadn't ever mentioned before surprised him. Long-lost friends, apparently.

The two bid each other farewell after exchanging phone numbers.

Billy checked on his father one more time. He was still sleeping. Betz grabbed his hand, giving it a squeeze. Parents represented strength and to see them differently was hard. It was difficult seeing a parent suffer.

On the way home, Billy talked about his regrets for not coming home more often. He should have. Work was always his excuse, the promotions he earned important to him.

He turned to Betz. "I want no more regrets. Life is too short. We're older now. Let's get married soon."

Betz replied. "There are details to work out. I have the children to think about."

"I know. It's important we include Annie and Will in any decisions we make that affect them. I've been doing quite a lot of thinking about our living situation," he said.

Betz turned, ready to say something.

"Please hear me out. We have not talked about it, I know. I'm sure you're expecting me to move into your house after we're married. It means no changes for the children. It's where you lived your whole life. However, I'm uncertain how I'd fit into a house their father was a part of. I'm not sure how accepting they'd be to that. We could also move into my father's house. He won't be returning there, obviously. I don't think the children would care for that either. It'd be like we took them out of their home and forced them into my life. I don't like that idea for anyone. What if we sell both houses? Move into one none of us have lived? It's a new life for all of us. Why shouldn't we start anew? I understand it will be different for the kids. Maybe they'll be excited about something unfamiliar." He looked at her sideways, not able to read her. "Honey, what are you thinking?"

"Hmmm, I have to think about this. It's a big decision."

"Give it some thought. We'll talk to the children before making a final decision. I want them to be part of the decision making."

"Thank you, Billy. I appreciate it. Annie will be driving soon. She'll be leaving home before we know it, but I need to make the best decision for everyone."

"That's what I want too. I just think buying a house together gives us that fresh start we're both looking for."

"I don't disagree. It's a lot, thinking about selling the only home I've known." Betz couldn't help being a little excited. The prospect of leaving the past behind and beginning anew was appealing.

Marj called the following week, asking Betz if she could meet her for lunch that day. It was short notice, but she had an appointment in Brimmer, and a rare free afternoon. Betz recently cut back her hours, working only four days a week, and it happened to be her day off. They agreed on what time to meet, giving Marj enough time to complete her commitments.

Betz was early, as usual. She selected a booth towards the back. She hadn't seen Marj in years. She wanted no interruptions. Betz waved to Marj as she entered the front door. Marj saw her, waving back. She walked briskly towards the booth, sliding into the seat opposite Betz. She placed her handbag next to her. The waitress came to take their order. Not ready to look at the menu yet, they both ordered coffee. The waitress wrote it down on her pad and walked away.

"Tell me everything." Both speaking at the same time. Laughing loudly, they received looks from others.

Marj signaled for Betz to go first.

Betz did not know where to start. She talked about how hard it was being a single mother to Annie while Kenneth was in South Korea.

"I love every minute of being a mother. Annie is so independent. So much like her grandmother," she said.

Tears came to her eyes when she shared her struggles during Will's illness. "He's a trooper," she said. "He's still slower than other children, but never complains. He'll live with the effects of polio for the rest of his life. He's a bookworm. I can't wait to see what his future will be."

"And Kenneth?" Marj asked.

When Betz told the story of Kenneth's accident, Marj was shocked. "You poor thing. You have been through a lot."

"What about you?" Betz asked.

"Once I left training here, I was lucky to receive a scholarship for nursing school in Milwaukee. My husband, Randy, agreed. He knew how much it meant to me. It required us to live apart until I graduated. We only saw one another on weekends."

"That must have been hard." Betz sympathized.

"It was. We postponed having a family until I completed my nursing degree. Once I graduated, I got a job at Oakwood. We delayed getting pregnant until I established myself. I needed to prove to the staff I was a good nurse. A baby would have complicated things. Randy agreed with me. Finally, after a year, we started trying. I had difficulty getting pregnant. Thank God I did. When my father took ill, any free time I had I spent caring for him. It was at his funeral when I overheard another couple talking. I overheard my husband was having an affair with one of the secretaries in his office."

Betz let out a loud gasp. "You've got to be kidding me?"

"Nope. I'm not. When I asked him about it, he admitted it. Apparently, it had been going on since my time going to nursing school. He said he didn't mean to hurt me. It just happened one night after having too many beers. She was consoling him. She felt sorry for him. I guess he was upset about me being away. He mentioned nothing to me during all that time. He explained he tried to end it when I was trying to get pregnant. He thought having a family would be the answer. When I couldn't get pregnant, both of us were disappointed. Then when my father became sick, I was at my job or taking care of him. He told me that is when their affair began again."

"That rotten animal." Betz couldn't help but say.

"Nah, Betz. I am partly to blame. I wasn't there for him like a wife should. He was kind enough to let me get my degree. I love the work that I do. It wasn't my fault I couldn't get pregnant or that my father took ill, but the rest of it…Yeah, I should have seen it coming."

"Wow, I'm at a loss for words."

"There's nothing to say. It was an amicable divorce. He married the secretary, by the way." She said it with a half-hearted laugh.

Marj continued. "I don't have any children, but lots of nieces and nephews to spoil. My mother just recently passed away. I moved into her house. It's big enough for me to take in boarders. An old family friend of my parent's recently took up residence. I've known him my entire life. He doesn't have any family in town and never married. It's nice having him around."

"May I ask? Is there a man in your life?

"Unfortunately, no. I've been too busy working and taking care of family."

"Speaking of family. I haven't told you about my unsuccessful search for my father over the years." Betz explained all the places she looked to find her father. She told her about the yellow rose placed on her mother's gravestone every year on her birthday. How the florist shared with her how an unidentified person paid cash for a single rose be delivered there for twenty years. "Those twenty years are up next year. I'm curious what will happen then. No one I know has admitted being the culprit. It's odd. I've always wondered if it may be my father."

"That is so romantic if it is. But why remain a mystery if it is him?" Marj said, implying she did not believe it was her father.

"Good point. Changing subjects. You never know if you'll meet someone. Look at me and Billy. I would never guess he'd come back in my life again. Maybe it'll happen for you too. By the way, can I ask your opinion on something?" Betz told her about the living options Billy proposed. "What do you think I should do?"

"I think you should get the children's opinion. Let them think they are part of the decision making, but persuade them it's time for changes. It's time to move out of your grandmother's house. I agree with Billy. To start over in a new house seems the best option for everyone.

"You're right. I'll talk to the kids."

Betz glanced at her watch. The afternoon had flown by. She needed to get home to prepare dinner.

"I'm sorry to say I've got to run. I'm so glad to see you again. I've enjoyed talking to you more than you know."

"I'm happy too. I've missed our talks. Let's do this again soon. Keep me posted about the house. I'm sure everything will work out."

"It will. Thanks."

Betz drove home, reflecting. She was lucky to have Marj as a friend. The years didn't seem to matter. Today was a reminder it's never too late to reconnect with someone. Look at her and Billy, and now Marj. Life was strange that way.

Excited to talk to Billy about the house, she waited until he called to tell him her decision. They'd talk to the children first. She decided the best thing would be to buy a house suitable for them to begin a new life together. Billy was ecstatic. It is what he wanted as well.

Billy arrived bearing gifts: flowers for Betz, a new LP record for Annie, a book for Will. It wasn't unusual as he often surprised them with presents. They were gathered in the living room before dinner when Billy spoke. "Annie, Will, your mother and I want your input. We want you to be part of a big decision we have to make."

Annie cringed, not knowing what was coming. Will leaned in a little closer, making sure he didn't miss a thing.

Betz began speaking. "We need to determine where to live once Billy and I are married."

Annie said, "But, I thought…"

Betz held up her hand to stop her. "Let me explain our options first." Betz carefully presented all three scenarios. She explained the pros and cons with each one.

"I know you may have assumed Billy would move in here. I'll tell you why that may not be the best choice." She kindly expressed how she felt Kenneth's, their father's, presence all around her. His touches were everywhere in this house.

"I don't think it's fair to any of us. Me, you two or Billy. This house is filled with memories. It's time we make new memories somewhere else. I've lived here my whole life. Some memories, I'm not so fond of." Betz talked more, explained more. She finished with, "I know this is a lot to hear. I want you to think about it. We don't have to decide tonight."

Annie couldn't believe what was happening. *Why did Billy come back?* Annie thought for sure her mother would marry Eugene. He was their father's friend, and she could tell he loved her mother. Eugene was there when their father died, and there for them, after. *He wouldn't have a problem moving into this house. Mother would never consider leaving here if she was marrying Eugene.*

Annie kept these thoughts to herself. Instead, she quickly stood up, walked over to her mother, and kissed her on the cheek. "Whatever you wish to do, Mama. Will and I are fine with it." She looked at Will, daring him to say anything different.

"Thank you, Annie," Betz whispered in her ear.

Annie knew her mother well. By the speech she just recited, she'd already decided. She was fine with it. She would never move into Billy's father's house, and her mother was right. She could not tolerate seeing Billy in places her father had dominated. The only other option was to move somewhere else.

She couldn't wait until she was old enough to leave.

Chapter 36

Billy contacted a real estate agent the next day. The agent had several houses in mind he thought they'd like. He was eager to show them.

Fortunately, it wasn't necessary for Betz to sell the house before they purchased another one. It gave Betz time to decide what to keep and what to get rid of. Billy did not want to rush the process, either. He wanted everyone to feel comfortable with the move.

They'd eventually sell Billy's family home, too. Now was not the proper time. Billy needed a place to live in the meantime. First, they'd find a new home. Once they accomplished that, they'd marry. Then place Betz's house for sale. Hopefully, the timing worked out and it would all fall into place. The important thing is to move together as a family.

On Saturday, Billy arrived, ready to take them house hunting. Betz couldn't contain her excitement. She was eager to do this. Will, nervous, climbed into the backseat. He wasn't sure what to expect, but kept his thoughts to himself. Annie, arriving last, slammed the car door after getting in. Betz looked at Billy and shrugged.

Billy turned around, smiling at them. "Are we ready to do this?" He didn't wait for their answer when he pulled away from the curb.

The first house the agent showed them was a big two story. The agent waiting on the front porch for them to arrive. When they were within hearing distance, he said, "Isn't this a beaut?" He ushered them through the front door, immediately pointing out the features of the home. Betz stood in the foyer. She immediately knew it wasn't the house for them. This house was too familiar, too much like the one they were living in. It was constructed in the same period. She winked at Annie when the agent told them it had good bones. Annie covered her mouth with her hand to prevent the giggles that threatened to erupt.

The tour over, they piled back into the car. Billy turned and said, "Sorry about that. I certainly hope he does a better job with the next one. I should have given him some guidelines."

Will became excited when they parked in front of the next house. The swimming pool, ice-skating pond and a baseball diamond were across the road. A park in the front yard. Even Annie looked impressed.

Mr. Nichols, the agent, once again began talking about the features of the house. "Now, this is what we call a split-level home. The houses on this street were all built similarly. That's because of the hill they sit on. As you can see from the outside, there is living space above the garage. Let's go inside, shall we?"

They entered a cute, cozy landing. They were met with a short set of stairs leading up, another leading down. Mr. Nichols led the way up first. When they reached the top, it opened into a large room with a fireplace on the opposite wall. Straight ahead was the kitchen. Betz couldn't believe how spacious it was. It had newer cabinets with an adorable eat-in dining area. Down the hallway were three bedrooms, with one large bathroom with two sinks.

Eyes widened as they walked downstairs. It was not what they were expecting to see. There was one large room for entertaining. A bar stood in the corner. A storage and utility room walled off on the opposite side.

"What do you think?" asked Mr. Nichols.

Betz looked at the kids. She read their excitement in their faces. "It's interesting," said Betz, not over enthusiastic. "It's not what I was picturing myself living in. I'd like to see a ranch house, please. One with rooms all on the same floor."

"Mama!" exclaimed Will.

Mr. Nichols stepped in. "The next one I have is exactly that."

They toured three more houses. All ranch style as Betz requested. Betz fell in love with one that had a double oven in the kitchen. Something she'd always wanted. It had a huge backyard with a willow tree. It was small, but Betz thought it would suit their family fine. It had been an exhausting day, touring all the houses. Billy drove over to Ruby's café to grab something to eat. After placing their order, Billy turned to Betz first.

"Which house is your favorite?"

"You know exactly which one I liked the most," she said with a grin. "The cozy ranch with the double ovens."

"Annie, what about you?" Billy asked.

"The second one. The split level."

"Will?"

"100% the one by the park."

Billy, being diplomatic, led a discussion of what each one offered. He was pleased how engaged the kids were, offering their input.

In the end, Betz gave in. The split level was a very nice house as well. The children seemed excited about moving there. That was more important to her than her double ovens.

They placed an offer on the house the next day. It was accepted the following day. Betz couldn't believe it. She was moving into a new home with her soon-to-be husband. She couldn't be happier that the kids were on board.

Cleaning out her childhood home was a daunting thought. Betz was unsure how she'd possibly get this done in time. Once again, Evelyn came to the rescue. She came on the next weekend with a plan. "We'll start with the attic," she said. "The guys can bring everything downstairs, so you can go through all of it. We'll label things. One for what you're taking with you, another for what is worth selling, another to give away, and the last will be for the trash. After the attic is completed, we'll move on to another room."

Betz hugged her. "Thank you. I don't know what I'd do without you."

Billy and Stuart hauled everything down from the attic. There was more there than expected. Evelyn began looking through boxes. Many items were of no use anymore. Items to be given away, old clothes, hats and small knick-knacks not worth anything.

Betz cautioned Evelyn to be watchful. "I've gone through almost everything here, but I don't want to miss anything that may pertain to my father."

"I know, my dear. I'll keep my eagle eyes open." Evelyn wiggled her eyebrows at her when she said this. Betz laughed at her silliness.

Evelyn shrieked when she opened a small shoebox inside a large box. Inside, she found dollar bills of different denominations.

"You're kidding me," Evelyn said as she flipped through the stack.

"I told you to be careful," Betz said, laughing at the expression on her friend's face.

The women determined which pieces of furniture could be sold. Many were not adequate for the new house. Billy had a couple of items from his family home he'd like moved. The pieces that held sentimental value to him.

The attic was only the first step. Encouraged by the headway made, it gave Betz the push she needed to complete the other rooms.

Later that evening, Betz broached wedding plans with Billy. She wanted to hear what he was thinking.

"All I want is to be with you in our new home," he declared.

She leaned over and kissed him. "You are the most wonderful man. Do you know that?"

"It's only because I'm telling you the truth," he said.

"I was thinking…maybe we should have a small church wedding. You've never been married. I never had a church wedding. I think it would be wonderful if Annie was my maid of honor," Betz said.

"And Will can be my best man. I love that idea. They might like me better if they take part."

"Will adores you and Annie just needs time. She's a teenager. She doesn't like anyone."

Billy laughed at that. "Go ahead, start making plans for a church wedding. Secure the date to correspond with us moving into the new house." He looked at her. "Have I told you lately how much I adore you?"

"I think it's been a while," she said before his lips met hers.

They pulled apart when they heard running on the stairs. Will rushed into the room, Annie following. "Annie says I have to get rid of all my books when we move. Is that true?"

Betz looked at Annie with a frown. "No, Will. It's not true. Be selective on what you decide to move but if you don't want to give up your books, we'll find space for them."

"I told you so," said Will.

Annie stuck her tongue out at her brother.

"Sit down, children. We have something to ask you."

Annie noticed her mother holding Billy's hand.

She turned to Annie. "Annie, my lovely daughter. Would you do me the honors of being my maid of honor? There is no other person I'd like standing next to me when we get married than you."

Tears sprang into Annie's eyes. She ran to her mother, throwing her arms around her. "Yes, please, yes."

"And Will," Billy said. "I can't think of anyone I'd rather have standing by me as my best man than you. What do you say?"

Will, more surprised than Annie at being asked, wholeheartedly agreed.

"Well, it's settled then."

Betz felt her life going at warped speed. She'd been able to secure the church for the date they wanted. She reserved a room at The Stardust, one large enough for the small reception afterwards. The dresses for her and Annie were currently being altered. Will's new suit was hanging in the closet upstairs.

Betz was still working amidst everything else. She continued sorting the items in the house, being careful to look through everything. Evelyn's money find was cause for being extra cautious.

Some things evoked too many memories. She couldn't bring herself to discard them. Thankfully, the new house had a big storage area. Plus, an attic to store things in.

One night, feeling depressed, she called Evelyn.

"What's wrong, dear?" Evelyn immediately heard something in her voice.

"It's my father. I got my hopes up again. I thought I'd discover something in the house."

"Oh, my poor girl. I don't know what to say. You've been looking for years. Your mother sure wanted to keep his identity a secret."

"I know. I don't understand why. What could have happened, do you think?"

"I wish I knew."

"I can't understand why I can't let it go," Betz said.

"Say, I read this somewhere. Why not write him a letter?" Evelyn's mind was churning. "Write to him every year on your birthday. Tell him whatever you need to tell him.”

“I have nowhere to send them.”

“That’s the point. You write how you’re feeling, place it in a box, and no one has to read it.”

Betz thought for a moment. “I guess it doesn’t hurt to try. I’m tired of feeling like this, wondering why I’m a secret.”

The night before her wedding, Betz sat down at the desk, and began writing.

Dear Father,

She stared at the words, willing herself to write more. The words escaped her. How was she to write a lifetime of questions and thoughts in a letter? She sat for the longest time. Sighing, she stood, folding the stationery in half. She placed it in one of her mother’s hatboxes she planned to keep. She’d try again someday.

Betz and Billy were married the following day. Annie looked beautiful in her new frock. Will stood proud next to Billy, looking all grown up.

The evening was filled with toasts to the lucky couple.

When the celebration ended, they drove to their new house on the hill where new memories would begin.

Chapter 37

It was Billy who taught Annie how to drive. Annie couldn't believe it when he suggested it one day. She didn't hesitate. He was kind and patient. He explained things, so she'd understand them. He treated her like a young adult, not a kid. When she messed up, he did not lose his patience. Instead, he kindly told her to try again. It was the first thing they'd done alone together. Annie was finding it easier to accept him into their family.

Annie became more independent than she'd been. It was the sixties. Drugs of all kinds were prevalent. Betz openly discussed the seriousness of trying drugs with both kids. She wasn't worried about Will. Annie was another story. When she broached the subject, Annie brushed her off, saying none of her friends do that. Betz peered at her, looking for any trace of a lie. To her relief, she didn't see any.

Annie was telling the truth. Her friends were not into the psychedelic drugs popular then. Liquor was their drug of choice. Every weekend, parties with alcohol were common, often on an isolated country road. Sometimes at a friend's house when parents were away. Her friends had no problem buying booze. Several had fake IDs, including Annie. They'd drive to a liquor store or country bar in a neighboring town where no one knew them to buy their alcohol.

One Saturday, Betz saw Annie leave the house. She yelled she was leaving as she ran down the sidewalk and hopped into the backseat of a white Chevy Corvair with baby moon hubcaps. She saw Gloria, Annie's friend, sitting in the passenger seat. Betz knew Gloria was dating Joey Churchill, a nice boy from a nice family. Betz heard Annie slam the car door shut. She wondered where they were off to tonight. Will interrupted her thoughts. Her mind shifting to his questions, with no more thoughts of Annie.

Tonight, the Corvair headed to a party out on Klondike Road. Joey, excited to get there, took a curve too fast. Bottles of PBR short necks rolled around in the car's front. The bottles clinking together. Earlier, Joey filled the trunk with two cases of beer and three bags of ice to keep them chilled. They all started laughing, hoping none of the bottles broke.

When they got there, four cars were already lined up. Joey parked and popped the trunk open. Everyone joked about the Corvair being a great drinking car. With the engine in the rear, the beer on ice was readily available to grab from the front trunk.

Joey yelled, "Good news, none of the shorties broke. Help yourself."

The radio was tuned into WLS, cranking out the latest tunes. As the night wore on, the music and voices grew louder. The evening was warm, the beer cold. Everyone was having a good time, Annie included. Unbeknownst to her, Annie was following in her grandmother's footsteps, Anneliese having done the same thing as her granddaughter was doing.

Annie's mother would certainly disapprove if she knew where she was and what she was doing.

The summer over, Annie began her senior year of high school. She had been accepted into the University of Wisconsin to study music. A dream she never thought would come true. Her music teacher wrote a letter of recommendation for her, proclaiming what a great vocalist she was and what a great addition to the program she'd be.

Annie already had a fake ID. They were easy to come by. Fortunately, the picture on hers actually looked like she did. Her friend Shelly, was another story. It wasn't even close to how she really looked. Every time she presented it, they held their breath, thinking they'd get caught and be in trouble.

A group of Annie's friends often traveled to a bar out of town. It was the only place to listen to live rock and roll music, something Annie couldn't get enough of. Her mother thought they were going to a popular pizzeria restaurant, oblivious to Annie's deception.

On one of the trips with the girls, Annie noticed a guy she had seen there before. She thought he was really cute. Annie couldn't stop looking at him. He eventually made his way over to her, introducing himself as Tommy Martin. Tommy was a sophomore at a college outside Chicago. Not wanting him to know how young she was, she told him she was attending college at Madison.

The live band playing was pretty good. Annie shared her love for music with him, telling him music was her major. When he told her he had seen The Doors at an outside concert, she became envious. Annie badly wanted to experience a concert herself and told him she was jealous. When it was time to leave, Tommy told her he'd hope to see her again. She hoped so, too.

Annie couldn't get the concert out of her head.

The summer after graduation, Annie read about the Woodstock Music Festival. It was predicted to be the largest outdoor music festival ever held. Many rock and roll and folk music groups were being featured. Annie wanted to go. The problem was it was in upstate New York. She tried convincing several friends to go with her. No one would commit. She was determined to go. She just needed to figure out how.

As August rolled around, the Woodstock festival grew near. One by one, Annie's friends came up with an excuse to why they couldn't join her. Annie was frustrated. One night she ran into Tommy again. They began talking about Woodstock. Annie shared her frustration and disappointment with the lack of interest her girlfriends had in attending the concert. Tommy, seeing her excitement for going, offered a solution.

"Hey, me and some friends are going. You're welcome to ride along. They won't mind. We're planning on taking a tent, sleeping bags and jugs of water. I read we can buy food on the grounds. We plan on packing only enough food for the ride there," Tommy said.

Annie couldn't believe it. Here was an opportunity to see top recording groups. One of the advertisements read 'Four Days of Peace and Music.' How could she pass this up?

"We're planning on returning home on Sunday. We aren't staying for the whole thing," he said. "What do you think, Annie? It'll be a blast!" Tommy was trying to convince her.

Annie, however excited, was a little apprehensive. Tommy was a sweet guy, but traveling hundreds of miles with someone she just met made her stop to think.

"I'd love nothing more than to go. It's a generous offer. I need to work some things out. How can I contact you?" Annie did not want him thinking she wasn't adventurous. She was. She wanted time to think this through. Her gut telling her it was fine. Her mind telling her she shouldn't go.

Tommy suggested they meet at the Pink Pony ice cream shop the following Saturday. Annie agreed.

She got to the Pink Pony early. Tommy was already in a booth with others. He introduced her to his friends. Everyone seemed really nice. She listened to them talk about the trip. They seemed to have it well planned out. As discussions continued, Annie became more and more comfortable with the idea of going.

One of the women turned to her, "Well, Annie, are you in?"

Not missing a beat, Annie replied she was.

Annie knew her mother would disapprove of her decision. She finally convinced her friend, Gloria, to go with. Her mother liked Gloria. She figured she'd be more open to the idea when she told her Gloria was going along. They would watch out for one another.

That evening, she broached the subject with her mother.

"Absolutely not," Betz said. "You can't go traipsing around the country like that."

"But Mama, I'm not going alone. I'm going with Gloria and a friend of hers." A white lie she thought she'd get away with. "Please. I want to do this. This will be my special experience before heading off to Madison for college."

Betz continued to say no.

When Billy got home that night, they were still arguing. Billy took Annie's side.

"Betz, let her go. Can't you see how much she wants this? If you don't give your approval, she'll more than likely go, anyway. She's almost eighteen. It'll be hard to stop her."

Reluctantly, Betz gave in. Annie's determination wore her down.

Betz second guessed herself when on Thursday afternoon, a VW mini-bus with a peace sign on its side pulled up at Annie's house. Betz hugged her daughter, uttering a word of caution as she walked out the door.

Annie jumped in the van, headed for an adventure of a lifetime.

It was a great time of year to drive across country. Music blared from the radio, and they were making great time. When they got closer to the Woodstock grounds, they were shocked at the traffic jams they encountered. When they got within five miles from the concert, traffic came to a standstill. Annie saw people leaving their vehicles and walking along the highway with bags on their backs. There was no movement in the traffic, and it became apparent they couldn't go any further. They'd have to leave the van and walk from here.

Tommy found a ditch off the road where he parked the van. Annie and the others jumped out. Annie, excited more than ever now that they arrived, was talking nonstop. They grabbed their sleeping bags, throwing their backpacks on their backs filled with items they thought they may need. They began making the long trek with hundreds of others to the concert site. It was slow going, and it seemed like it was taking forever. The surrounding scene was beyond anyone's imagination.

As they got closer, they heard music blasting through huge speakers scattered throughout the grounds. When they entered the gate, they were shocked at the number of people already there. There were thousands of kids everywhere you looked.

Tommy found a spot on the hillside to set up camp. They erected the tent, throwing their things inside. By the time they finished, the musicians were performing on stage. Tommy and the others sat together on the ground, absorbing the music with those around them. Annie hugged Gloria.

"We're going to remember this for the rest of our lives. Thank you for coming with me," Annie whispered to her.

The crowd grew larger than expected during the afternoon. The people kept coming. Some trampling over the fences, knocking them down as they tried to get in. Word was quickly spreading about the concert. Annie heard them announce over the loudspeaker that the concert was now free-of-charge. "Come one, come all," they said. The gates were now open to everyone.

It wasn't until much later when they introduced Melanie up on stage. As she began singing "Beautiful People," Annie looked around at the people dancing and singing along. She'd witnessed nothing like this before. Women and men alike were not inhibited from displaying their free spirits.

Joan Baez was the last performer that night. When she sang "Swing Low, Sweet Chariot," Annie thought she'd died and went to heaven. It moved Annie to tears.

Sleeping in the tent was challenging, too many people, too little room. A couple of guys took their sleeping bags outside until a light, steady rain began to fall during the night. They hurried back into the tent to keep dry. Everyone moved closer together to make room for them. No one minded. They were grateful for the body heat keeping them warm from the cold, damp night.

When they woke the next morning, the guys went to find food. They came back with nothing, telling them the vendors ran out the previous night. Thankful to have eaten when they had the day before, they grabbed snacks from their backpacks. It wasn't much, but at least it was something.

A steady drizzle began, making the ground wet. They had to take turns going to the bathroom. If they didn't, they'd lose their spot on the grass where they were sitting. It was that crowded. On one of the trips there, Annie saw a pregnant woman being helped to the medic tent. It looked like she was struggling and

Annie couldn't help but think how crazy it was she was here.

When Creedence Clearwater Revival began playing, Annie gave herself a reality check. It was one of her favorite bands. She was actually here, at a live concert, listening to musicians she heard on the radio playing on a stage in front of her. It was surreal.

One of the guys in the group next to them, lit up a joint and passed it to them. Tommy immediately took a hit and passed it on. Annie watched the others do the same. She never smoked pot before, but when it came her turn, there was no hesitation on her part. Annie let the feeling of freedom flow through her body as she partook and became one with the music throughout the night.

They agreed they'd leave on Sunday, but the music and the atmosphere changed their minds. They didn't want to leave even though the rain was coming down, and they were soaking wet. People were slipping and sliding in the mud. Everything was a mess. The rain delayed the bands from playing on schedule, but it was a beautiful place to be.

On Monday morning, Annie was awakened to the sound of a guitar. When the group climbed out of the tent, they heard Jimi Hendrix playing his version of 'The Star-Spangled Banner'. It was 9am in the morning and it was an absolutely amazing performance. Annie was in awe.

They listened to a few more songs before packing it up and hiking back to the van. Exhausted, the trip home was quiet, letting those who could catch up on their sleep.

When Tommy pulled up to Annie's house everyone hugged good bye. Annie couldn't thank Tommy enough for letting her tag along.

"You gave me a lifetime of memories," she said fondly. "That was quite the experience for this small-town girl."

Tommy laughed.

Betz was waiting for her when she entered the house. Annie briefly told her mother about the wonderful performances she saw and the music she heard during her time at Woodstock. She kept the other details to herself.

In later years, Annie realized no one would understand her experience that weekend unless they were there. It was indescribable.

A week later, the family drove Annie to Madison. Betz wondered where the time went. It seemed impossible her firstborn was going away to college.

After getting Annie settled into her dorm room, they walked around campus. The Memorial Union, Bascom Hall and most important to Annie, Music Hall were just a few of the buildings they visited. The campus was quite impressive, and Betz was glad Annie chose this university to spend the next four years at.

Betz looked at her child. Annie was ready for the next phase of her life. Betz wasn't sure if she was.

Chapter 38

Betz woke with anticipation. Today, was her mother's birthday. Billy joked with her the night before about it being her twenty-first. It was in a way. This year marked the twenty-first anniversary of her death. Would this be the year the florist no longer placed the rose on her mother's grave? Twenty years had already passed. Today, she'd know if the person responsible for the yellow rose still remembered her mother.

She declined Billy's offer to go with her. She wanted to stop by Kenneth's grave first. Plus, she wanted to do this alone. She wasn't sure what her reaction would be. If no rose appeared on the gravestone, it meant an end to an era. If there was a rose present, it meant the mystery continued. A mystery that drove Betz wild.

Billy didn't want his wife to get her hopes up. Betz believed the rose was in some way connected to her father. He wasn't convinced of that, but didn't discourage her fantasizing about it. Betz stopped looking for her father after Billy and her married and moved into their new home. She had renewed hope of discovering something when they packed everything up, but when she came up empty-handed, she decided her continued search was futile. The chances of finding anything was gone.

It was midafternoon when Betz made her way to the cemetery. She didn't visit the grave as often as she did in the past, but always visited on the anniversary of her mother's death and her birthday. She walked slower than normal. Subconsciously, not wanting to know the answer to a question she desperately needed.

As she walked the path she'd walked for years, she started becoming anxious, and quickened her pace. When she neared the tombstone, she unknowingly let out a breath she didn't realize she was holding. There it was, once again, a yellow rose.

She kneeled on the grass and picked up the rose, placing it underneath her nose. She closed her eyes and breathed in the fresh scent. Her imagination raced. This meant the person was still alive. So many thoughts went through her mind, much like it did every year. But this year was different. After twenty years, someone continued to remember Anneliese, her beloved mother. *Who was this person? Where did they live?* It was useless to ask the florist again. They'd tell her the same story. The person remained a mystery.

Betz placed the rose back where she found it. She began pulling weeds around the granite, amazed at how quickly they grew. When she completed the task, she sat in the grass, resting her back against the stone. With no one around, she began talking.

She talked about Annie being in college, doing well. They were shocked to learn Mr. Bailey from Bailey Oil Company had set aside college funds for both Annie and Will in honor of Kenneth. Annie was loving her music major and Betz wondered how she was going to use her degree when she finished. Betz hoped Annie would stay away from the Vietnam War protests. But knowing Annie…Betz didn't finish that thought.

How proud she was of Will. He was in the top ten of his class. He was unsure what he'd major in or what college he'd attend, but she was confident he'd find his way. His muscle weakness never quite went away, but he dealt with it.

Billy seemed to like his job. He just got another promotion. The company was impressed with his knowledge and experience he brought from Chicago. It was an opportunity they never expected to have. The timing was right when a glass company built a factory in the neighboring town shortly after Billy moved back.

She told her mother about the job at the hospital. How it still fulfilled her. How appreciative patients were for her help. She felt useful, and that she made a difference.

She was worried about Billy's father. He wasn't doing well. She was planning on visiting him this week. She wanted to see her friend, Marj too. She still worked at the nursing home where Harold was.

Betz stood. It was time to go.

"Well, Mother, another year has passed. The mystery continues. Happy Birthday!"

She straightened her clothes before setting off towards her car. She had noticed the beautiful butterfly lingering near the flowers all the while she sat there, talking to her mother. Strangely enough, it followed her all the way to her car before disappearing.

She sat in the car for a moment, trying to decide how she felt. It wasn't as if she wanted the rose to disappear. Then she realized she was bitter. For someone to not identify themselves was preposterous, unfair.

Betz drove home in a daze. When she arrived, Billy was not home yet. She needed to talk to someone. Evelyn picked up on the fourth ring. Betz rambled on about the yellow rose, barely stopping to take a breath. When she came up for air, Evelyn finally spoke. She empathized with Betz, but scolded her at the same time.

"You should have prepared yourself for this. What made you think the appearance of the rose would suddenly stop?" She kindly reminded her. "When you feel this way, write that letter, share your thoughts. If you think it is your father, put in words what you'd say to him. Tell him how you're feeling." Evelyn was very blunt with her.

Billy reiterated Evelyn's suggestion when he got home. Since there was no way to identify the person, she needed to release her agitated feelings. A letter may help.

When Marj called that evening, she told her the yellow rose appeared once again.

"After twenty years," Betz said.

"It simply means the person is still alive. It doesn't tell you who that person is. Who knows whose life your mother touched when she was alive? It may be no one you'd expect. It's nice she is being remembered." Marj tried to make light of the subject.

No one understood. It was driving Betz mad not knowing who this person was. Regardless, she sat at the desk that evening with pen and paper in front of her. She sat there, thinking of what she wanted to say. She began.

Dear Father, I

Once again, the words wouldn't come. She sat there. Her thoughts jumbled together. Frustrated, she folded the paper and placed it into the hatbox with the others.

Someday, maybe she'd be able to write her thoughts.

Chapter 39

Unsure where the years went, Betz sat, reflecting on her life and the lives of her children.

Annie had graduated from state university in Madison years before. To Betz's horror, she became involved in the Vietnam protests common on campus. Thankfully, she was never arrested or hurt. Annie told her she couldn't stand by and do nothing. The war was not worth it and too many young people were dying.

After college, Annie never left the area, and remained living in the suburbs of the great city she came to love. Her music degree landed her a job as a teacher at a middle school. Encouraging students to explore music as an alternative to other extracurricular activities became her focus. She was impacting young lives without knowing it, and Betz could not be prouder.

On the weekends, Annie was the lead singer in the band, 'Splash.' It was a cover band, playing old rock and roll tunes of the sixties and seventies. That is how she met, her husband, James. He was the drummer. James loved to tell the story how Annie was not impressed with him when they first met. He claims it was love at first sight.

The two were married in a park along Lake Mendota at sunset. It was a simple wedding. No frills, which fit Annie to a tee. It was absolutely breathtaking, watching the sun go down, casting an orange glow over the water as they said their vows. After the reception, Annie took center stage, with microphone in hand. Betz placed her hands over her heart when she began singing. Her daughter had the most beautiful voice she had ever heard. Of course, being her mother, she was a little prejudice.

After playing a few songs, Annie led James to the dance floor. The lead guitarist began strumming his acoustic guitar, as Annie began singing *Dance with Me,* holding James' hand as she looked into his eyes. When she sang the line about wanting to be your partner, James pulled her close and kissed her. She had picked the perfect love song for musicians.

It was a memorable night with the band playing until midnight. Everyone enjoying themselves immensely.

Annie and James now had three beautiful children, a house, a dog, a life they built together.

Will followed his sister to the University of Wisconsin, Madison. He met his lovely wife, Madeline, his senior year. The first time Betz met her she sensed she was a perfect match for her son. Will, always serious, Madeline gregarious, funny, and kind. It thrilled Betz when she found out she was getting her degree in nursing, something Betz never managed to achieve.

Their marriage ceremony took place in a beautiful church. One Madeline's family had attended for generations. It was a wonderful sight, seeing Will standing at the altar.

Betz reflected how scared she'd been when Will was young, becoming afflicted with polio. He'd fought so hard. They all did, but they'd overcome the obstacles. There were times Will still struggled. He never knew what may trigger his muscle weakness. It was something he'd have to live with the rest of his life. It was another reason Betz was grateful Madeline was a nurse.

Will was an architect, working for a well-known firm. Madeline, a nurse at a large hospital. They never left the Madison area either. Madeline's parents lived close by, helping with their two gorgeous children.

Annie did not live far from her brother. Betz's dream of a houseful of children finally coming true when the two families got together. It was chaotic and loud, but Betz loved every minute of it.

Chapter 40

Betz's career for the last thirty years had been amazing. She'd given a lot of thought to the idea of retiring. There had been many discussions with Billy and her friends regarding when the right time was. She was now in her sixties. It was getting harder to move patients around. She no longer had the same strength she used to. Her knees ached from being on her feet all day. Her body wasn't the same as it was when she was younger. It was time.

Betz glanced at herself in the bathroom mirror. She traced the wrinkles around her eyes with her fingers. She outlined her lips with the tube of lipstick, selecting Pink Passion from the others. Today, would be her last day putting on her uniform. Her final day working with the doctors and nurses she came to love. She'd miss working with the patients. Mostly, they had been wonderful people to care for. Of course, throughout the years, she had her share of ill-tempered ones. Some she'd rather forget.

It was the right decision, and the right time to retire. She wasn't getting any younger, and she wanted to spend more time with her grandchildren.

Betz looked at herself in the full-length mirror. She didn't look bad for a woman in her late sixties. A few pounds heavier, with a few more wrinkles.

She drove to the hospital, feeling nostalgic. When she stepped into the nurses' lounge, she was greeted with shouts of congratulations. A banner hung above the sofa with the words "Happy Retirement" on it. A cake sat in the middle of the table, waiting to be cut. Betz was amazed at the number of people who stopped by to acknowledge her. She'd miss this cohort of people. Work became more than just a job to her. It had served her well. There were tears as she said goodbye to the people she worked with for years.

Billy arrived home early with a bottle of champagne to celebrate. They laughed when he popped the cork. The sound making them both jump. He poured each of them a glass of the bubbly, making a wonderful toast to his wife. He loved her still after all these years.

Betz teared up with the kind, thoughtful words her husband said about her. She was a lucky woman. She couldn't be happier.

Billy continued working at the glass company. He was not ready to retire yet. "Soon," he kept telling her.

They still lived in the same house they bought when they married. They began traveling once the kids left, having fewer commitments. Betz never realized how much she enjoyed venturing to other parts of the country. There was so much to see. Often, they'd travel with Evelyn and Stuart, the four remaining great friends. In recent years, their trips became less and less frequent. Instead, she traveled to Madison to see the grandkids. Betz hoped to visit more often now that she wasn't working.

Life was good. There were lots to be thankful for. Her kids were healthy and happy. She remained in love with her husband, her husband loving her back. She had everything a person would want. Yet, there remained an emptiness she couldn't describe.

Betz continued visiting her mother's gravesite. The mysterious yellow rose still appearing on her birthday.

Over the years, Betz tried to rid herself of the hole in her heart. The unfinished letters she continued to write filled the hatbox. Every year she promised herself she'd do it. Every year, the words never progressed beyond,

Dear Father, I

What was holding her back? Why couldn't she release her feelings? Why did she still want to know?

Chapter 41

Betz took advantage of her retirement and made several trips to Madison. She felt blessed for the chance to spend time with the children, to see them in their own element. She made plans to have the grandchildren spend a couple of weeks with her in the summer. She was excited for them to come to Brimmer. She had already planned things for them to do.

Betz often went shopping with Evelyn or had lunch with Marj. Betz continued to see Marj whenever she visited Harold, Billy's father, at the nursing home. Once Harold died, they continued their friendship that began years before.

Marj was trying to convince Betz to volunteer at the rest home. They needed the help, and it would give her something to do.

"Just volunteer one day a week," Marj begged. "Don't you miss helping patients?"

Betz admitted she did. Betz was getting a little bored when she remained home all week. She hadn't agreed yet, though she was tempted. It sounded appealing.

The two women had a lot in common. Marj was so easy to talk to.

Evelyn was Betz's childhood friend, her best friend. Evelyn knew everything about her life, all her childhood dreams, her habits, everything. She'd been there for her since grade school. They'd remain friends forever.

Marj was her adulthood friend, if that made sense. She entered her life later, yet she felt like she'd known her forever.

One day, Marj called her. She asked if she was free to meet. She wanted to talk to her. She sounded upset, so Betz invited her to come to the house.

Marj arrived an hour later. Betz led her into the family room, inviting her to sit. It was unlike Marj to look so frazzled.

"Marj, whatever is wrong? I'll fetch us some coffee."

"I need something much stronger than coffee. You have any whiskey?"

"Of course." Betz walked to the liquor cabinet, grabbing two glasses. She ventured to the kitchen for ice. She glanced at the clock hanging on the wall. It was 1:30 in the afternoon. *Something must really be wrong. S*he thought. She reentered the room, pouring whiskey over the ice, and handed the glass to Marj. She took a large gulp, then coughed.

"Oh my, that stuff is strong," she said.

Betz refrained from laughing. Marj's face indicated this was serious. Instead, she took a small sip of her drink, waiting for Marj to begin.

Marj took another swig. This time a wee smaller, not making her cough.

"Are you ready for this?" she began.

"I'm not sure. I don't know what it is yet," replied Betz.

Marj said nothing. Betz waited for her to continue.

"I'm about to tell you an unbelievable story."

Betz took another sip of her drink. She thought it best to say nothing, to let Marj talk at her own pace.

Marj sighed before proceeding. "I've already told you about the house boarder I took in."

Betz remembered this tidbit. He'd lived there for years.

"I've known him my whole life." Tears sprang into Marj's eyes. "He's a family friend. He was always invited to every holiday or celebration we had. I always felt sorry for him. He never married. It was like my family took it upon themselves to make him part of our family."

Betz wasn't sure where this story was leading. She thought maybe something happened to him. He was old. She wasn't sure how old. She thought he had to be close to his nineties. "Is he ok?" Betz asked. "Did something happen to him?" If Marj lost her family friend, she knew it would be devastating to her.

Marj gave a look of horror. "No, he's not. He had a heart attack right in front of me."

"Oh no, what happened?" Betz asked in disbelief.

"We were having dinner when he grabbed his chest. He fell off the chair. I ran to him. I panicked. I had the sense to call Emergency before I began resuscitation. I immediately began CPR. It seemed like it took forever before I heard the sirens. I'm unsure how long I worked on him."

"Oh, my goodness! Did he survive?"

"Yes. The rescue squad finally arrived. When they took over the resuscitation, I fell over backwards in exhaustion."

"Oh, Marj. That's awful. I'm so sorry. He's lucky you were there. How is he now?"

"He's stable. They say I saved his life."

"I'm sure you did."

Marj raised her finished whiskey glass to Betz. "Another, please?"

Betz complied. She couldn't imagine the trauma Marj experienced. When she handed Marj a full glass of whiskey, Marj thanked her.

"That's not all," she whispered.

Betz feared the worse. She thought Marj was about to say he died in the hospital after she saved him.

"He thought he was going to die," Marj continued. "I was sitting there, alongside his hospital bed, when he woke. He motioned me to come closer."

Betz leaned in closer, towards Marj in order to hear her.

"You know what he said to me?"

"He thanked you for saving his life?" Betz guessed.

"Huh, no… You will never believe what I'm about to tell you."

"Not in my wildest dreams."

"He told me I am his blood. I thought he was delirious. I told him I know. He is a member of our family. He turned to me. Eyes glued to mine."

He said, "No, you don't understand. You are my daughter. Betz, the look in his eye. I can't explain. It was like he was telling me the truth," Marj said.

Betz, flabbergasted had nothing to say.

"I didn't believe him, of course. He just had a heart attack. He was medicated."

"Impossible. It can't be true. He was only wishing for the family he never had," said Betz.

"Betz, I'm not finished. He told me the whole story. How he and my mother were high school sweethearts. How he loved her his entire life. How he tried to stay away from her. How the two had an affair. How my father never suspected, never knew. He raised me like I was his own. He said there was no proof, but my mother swore to him it was true. My brother, Paul, is his son too. Can you believe it? My brother is going to blow a gasket when he finds out. He never felt part of the family. That's why he moved to California. His two older brothers never accepted him. How do I tell him?"

Not waiting for Betz to comment, Marj continued her story. "He swore to my mother he would never tell a soul. She wanted Paul and me to believe the father who raised us was our true father. He promised her never to reveal the secret. Even after her death, he kept his promise. I asked why he told me now. His response broke my heart. I've loved you like a daughter. You've taken care of me like a father. I thought it time you heard the truth before it's too late."

Betz felt like she was watching a movie. *Oh, the tangled webs we weave* was a thought that came to her mind.

"Betz, Betz?"

Betz pulled out of her reverie.

She needed to be here for her friend. However, she was speechless. What advice could she give? She, for years, longing for a father so badly. Marj now learning she had two. The one who raised her and the one who gave her birth.

"Marj, whether or not you believe it, you have been given a gift. You know your truth. Embrace it."

Marj hugged her friend. "Betz, I've treasured our friendship. Thank you. Thank you for being here. I don't know who else I would have shared this with."

The two continued to talk until Billy came home.

"What have we here?" asked Billy.

"Nothing." Marj and Betz responded in unison.

"You two." Billy said as he shook his head. "It's uncanny how you respond simultaneously."

"I'll fill you in later," Betz said.

Billy raised his eyebrows at Betz when he noticed the absence of whiskey in the decanter. The unspoken words between husband and wife were enough. She'd relay to him what transpired later. For now, he'd leave the two women alone.

Marj left shortly after.

Betz filled Billy in on the revelation.

They both agreed life was full of curve balls. Marj's recent discovery of her birth father was one for the books.

Betz was conflicted. She empathized with Marj. Everything she grew up with was a lie. She understood that. However, she'd give anything for her father to reveal himself.

The more time elapsed, the more unlikely she knew that was.

Chapter 42

Betz stayed in close contact with Marj over the following weeks. Her father continued to improve from his heart condition. He was being released from the hospital. No longer needing the critical care of medical staff.

Betz met Marj for lunch. They grabbed a table and placed their order.

"How are you doing?" Betz asked her friend.

"I'm doing fine."

"Truthfully." Betz grabbed Marj's hand across the table, reassuring her true feelings were safe with her.

"I'm getting used to the idea. The man I considered my parent's friend is my father. Saying it out loud sounds ridiculous." Marj snickered under her breath. "I've asked him a lot of questions. He's been pretty forthcoming. He claims he's loved my mother since he was a teenager. He swears he accepted her marrying someone else. They remained friends, and only friends. Then one day he saw my mother upset about something. Then one thing led to another. I'm the result from that something. He says he never had a clue he was my father until my brother was born. He promised my mother he'd tell no one he was our birth father. He kept his promise until he couldn't."

"How is your brother taking the news?" Betz asked.

"Not well. He wants nothing to do with him. He claims he's made his life miserable for not coming forward sooner. My brother was never accepted by my older siblings. Maybe they suspected something, who knows?"

"Did they treat you differently?"

"Never. I don't understand that. I've always felt sorry for Paul for the way he was treated."

"You know, this is a wild story. One that's hard to comprehend."

"I know. It's unbelievable. It makes me wonder if he hadn't had a heart attack would he have ever told me?"

"I wonder." Betz said.

"I'm no longer angry. I had a wonderful childhood. My father, not my birth father, loved me. My life would have been messy if I'd found out sooner."

"I'm torn," Marj admitted. "I'm not sure what to do. My father, wow, that's strange to say. My father is ready to go home from the hospital. I'm a nurse. I can care for him, but I'm still working. He's ninety-one. I'm thinking he'd do better in the nursing home. I can look after him there. What do you think?"

"Marj, I think that's a wise decision. You'd worry leaving him by himself during the day."

"My thoughts exactly. I feel guilty, though. His last days in a nursing home? I'm afraid he may think it's because of what he's told me."

"If you explain you can be with him every day, he'll understand. He has no other family, does he?

"No, just me and my brother that I'm aware of."

"Don't second guess yourself. It's the right choice for everyone."

"Thanks, Betz. I can always count on you. Have you given thought to volunteering? I'd get to see you more. I hear they need help to monitor the social room. You'd be great at that."

"Maybe." Betz said. "I've been considering it."

"Please do. It is not a big commitment, only one day a week. Someone can cover you when you go see the kids. Come on, it'll be fun."

"We'll see."

The two women finished their lunch and said goodbye.

"Call me. Let me know how your father adjusts." Betz said before climbing into the driver's seat.

Betz thought about Marj's suggestion for an entire week. She discussed volunteering at the nursing home with Billy.

"Honey, you've been talking about it for a while. There is no harm in trying it. If you don't like it, then quit," he said.

"I'm worried about the commitment. I don't want it to interfere with anything we'd do together or the children."

"Make that clear when you volunteer. They will be grateful for the help. No matter the time you have."

"You're right. I'll do it."

Betz began volunteering. She enjoyed it. She didn't realize how much she missed interacting with others. It'd already been a couple of weeks now since she began overseeing the social room. She had yet to meet Marj's father. His hospitalization had left him weaker than they anticipated. They were keeping a close eye on him. He kept to himself in his room.

One night, Marj called, crying. "Betz, it's my father. He's contracted pneumonia. He's not doing well. I should have never admitted him to the nursing home."

"It has nothing to do with it, Marj. He had a heart attack. He's old. You know better than anyone, pneumonia is not uncommon for elders. Stop blaming yourself."

"I know, but I can't help it. I feel bad."

Betz finally convinced her it was inevitable. "He will not live forever."

Marj was checking on her patients when she peeked into her father's room. The pneumonia had not improved. He slept more than he was awake. When she cracked the door open, she was surprised to see him sitting in bed, alert. He saw her, beckoning her to come in.

Marj came into the room. "What can I get you?"

"How bad is it? Please tell me the truth." It was difficult to talk. He was out of breath.

"Your prognosis is not good." Marj wished the doctors were here to explain.

"How long?"

"Not long." Marj squeezed his hand. "I won't leave you. I'll be here."

"There's something I need to tell you." he said.

Marj's heart dropped. She didn't think she was ready for whatever he was about to say.

"Please. This is important."

Marj held her breath. "Go on."

A coughing fit prevented him from continuing. Marj handed him a glass of water with a straw. He took a drink. The coughing stopped.

"There was another woman besides your mother," he managed to say.

Marj slowly set the glass she was holding back down.

"It's a long story. In the end, she no longer wanted to see me. I loved her too in my own way. I never forgot her. Each year, on her birthday, I've had a yellow rose placed at her gravesite."

Marj sat back in her chair, speechless. Her father leaning back in the pillows, eyes half closed.

"There's one more thing," he said. "She had a baby. My baby."

Marj couldn't catch her breath. She thought she was about to have a panic attack. She waited for more. His eyes already closed, his breathing becoming deeper. He had fallen asleep.

Marj quietly left the room. She slipped into the bathroom and splashed water over her face. She found a quiet place to sit. The chair faced a large window overlooking the woods surrounding the building, a view she never came to appreciate. Today, she was hoping it'd settle her nerves.

Marj replayed her father's words in her mind. She suddenly jumped from her chair. *It can't be. It's more than a coincidence.*

Marj walked swiftly down the hall towards the recreation area. She couldn't remember what day it was. When she opened the double doors, she was relieved to see Betz. She motioned for her to come with her. Betz swept the room with her hand, telling her without words, she couldn't leave.

Marj grabbed her by the hand.

"What's going on?" Betz asked.

Marj did not say a word but kept walking. She took a deep breath before pushing the door open to the room, she just left minutes before.

Betz saw a patient lying groggily against the pillows with his eyes open.

Marj squeezed her hand harder. "Betz, meet your father."

Betz looked at her, bewildered. Marj nodded.

The eyes staring at her were identical to hers. There was no mistaking it.

She'd waited for this day her entire life.

Chapter 43

Betz's heart clamored in her chest. She looked between Marj and the man lying there. Marj pulled her closer to the bed.

"Mack, this is Betty Ann Doyle. Betz, this is Mack. I believe he is the father you've been looking for all these years."

"Doyle? Your mother. Was her name Anneliese?" You can tell he was struggling to talk.

"Yes, Anneliese was my mother." Betz dropped her voice to a whisper. Tears sprang to her eyes as she asked him. "Are you really my father?"

Mack turned his head towards the wall. Silence stretched on before he answered. "If you are Anneliese's daughter, Betty, then yes I am."

Marj caught Betz as she staggered backwards. Betz thought she would be sick. She couldn't stop looking into Mack's eyes. A chair was thrust behind her, forcing her to sit. Marj took a chair and sat next to her. The tears in both their eyes silently sliding down their faces.

A series of coughing broke the spell. Mack's lungs continued to fill with fluid. The doctors were powerless to help him. He looked over at the two women sitting next to him. They deserved to know the truth.

Mack began his tale.

"I've made mistakes. I've hurt people. I don't deny it. I've loved two women in my life. They both swore me to secrets I've kept for years. I've sacrificed a lot for those secrets, but no longer. It's time for the truth." His breathing was becoming more labored.

"Marjorie, I'm sorry I waited so long to tell you I'm your father. There were many times I wanted to. I'm so grateful to be part of your life since the day you were born. Your brother, as well. It hurt me to the core whenever I was referred to as a family friend. I am your father, dammit." When his voice raised an octave, another bout of coughing came. When it was over, he continued.

"Marj, your mother, Rosalie, and I were high school sweethearts. We loved each other. When I returned from the war, she had married someone else. George Walsh was a great guy. I liked him and we all became friends. We built and managed a lumber store together for years. When your mother confided in me, they were having some marriage difficulties, that's when we began having an affair. It ended shortly after it began. We knew it was wrong, and we didn't want to hurt, George."

Mack's voice was getting raspy. Marj offered him a drink of water. He took a tiny sip, eager to continue telling his story.

"One night at a holiday gala, I met a beautiful woman." He turned to Betz. "Your mother, Anneliese. It was great timing. I needed to move on with my life, get married, have a family of my own. I began falling in love with her. Then, her father died. She had little time for me. She was grieving and taking care of her mother. It was a tumultuous time.

She was very close to her father, your grandfather. She was devastated by his death."

Betz drew in a breath at the mention of her mother.

Mack hesitated, but explained. "I never intended to have another affair with your mother." He was looking at Marj. "It just happened one night when she was upset with your father again. A mistake on both our parts." Mack looked despondent when he admitted to the affair.

"A few months later, Anneliese came to me. She told me she was pregnant with our child. I proposed to her. I wanted a wife and family. I was falling in love with her and knew we'd be good together, but I felt guilty. So, I told her about my affair with Rosalie. She was understanding, telling me everyone makes mistakes. We continued making wedding plans."

They were interrupted by the doctor coming into the room.

"Mr. Connolly, I suggest you rest. Your vitals aren't where they should be. You're exerting yourself too much."

Mack waved him away. "This is important. More important than my vitals."

The doctor who knew Marj looked at her and shrugged. They both understood rest would only give him a little more time, anyway. Mack closed his eyes after he left. He wasn't proud of his next revelation.

"When I told Rosalie I was getting married, she told me she was carrying my child. Not only that, she threw me another bombshell. She told me I was your father, Marjorie. She made me swear George would never be told. Nobody would have knowledge of this. Though it pained me, I knew your mother was right. I couldn't hurt your father, my best friend, my business partner like that. Your mother convinced me it was best for the children. I agreed."

Mack stopped for a moment.

"Betty, I thought I was doing right by telling your mother about being the father of Rosalie's children. I was wrong. She wanted nothing to do with me. She didn't trust me. She said she'd raise the baby on her own. I tried reaching out to her, but she never responded. I found out your name was Betty Ann. I put money into an account for you each month until you turned eighteen. Did you know that? I went to your school once to get a glimpse of you. It upset me so much knowing I'd never get to meet you, so I never returned."

It was getting more difficult for Mack to speak. He was almost finished.

"When I heard your mother died of cancer, I almost reached out to you, but remembered my promise to her. I couldn't break that promise. I had a yellow rose placed on her tombstone every year on her birthday. I wanted her to know how much I had cared for her. For me, it was my way of showing my love. Regrets, I have so many regrets."

Betz and Marj both sat at his side, listening to his story with tears flowing down their cheeks. This man was far from perfect. His decisions cost him dearly. Yet, he was still their father.

Mack's body went lax when he finished his tale. The toll on his mind and body a relief. The truth expelled from his body exhausting.

"Girls, please forgive me. Betz, I have thought of you every day since you were born. You were not forgotten. Marj, thank you for all you've done for me. You have given me great joy. You have been a wonderful friend to me. I only wish I could have called you, my daughter."

Sobbing, Betz leaned over and kissed him on the cheek. "I forgive you," she said.

Mack was holding onto dear life. His health failing rapidly. His breathing becoming more ragged. It was becoming harder to breathe. He hoped he'd done the right thing, revealing the truth. There was one more thing to say. "I love you both more than words can say."

Mack's body suddenly relaxed. He took his last breath with both daughters holding a hand.

Betz's body wracked with sobs. She couldn't let go. She'd just found him. Now he was gone.

Marj walked over to her side of the bed. "Betz," she said as she helped her to her feet.

They held each other tight. "Sister, it's time to go," Marj quietly said.

Betz stiffened her back.

"What?" asked Marj.

"Oh, my goodness! We're sisters!" Betz exclaimed.

"Yes, dear friend. You are my sister. I couldn't have chosen a better one."

Betz grabbed Marj and hugged her tight. "You don't know what this means to me. I've always wanted a sibling."

"I think I do," Marj responded.

Chapter 44

It was in the middle of the night when Betz snuck downstairs. With pen and paper in hand, she sat down to write her final letter. She had so much to say. She began, as she always did.

Dear Father,

This time, the words flowed without effort. When she finished, she carefully folded the edges, placing it into the hatbox for the last time. A sense of tranquility overcame her. The missing piece finally filling the gaping hole in her heart. The knowledge of who she was completing her. She felt whole for the first time in her life.

The search was over.

The End

Afterword

Upon my retirement, I became interested in my family's genealogy. I wanted to know my roots, where my ancestors originated from. I was delighted to learn I was a Mayflower descendent not only of William Bradford, Governor of Plymouth, but Richard Warren and Samuel Fuller who also sailed on the Mayflower and signed the Mayflower Compact.

Excited by what I found; I urged my husband to let me research his family's genealogy as well. He was reluctant. He knew nothing about his maternal grandfather, and wasn't sure he wanted to find out. I wanted to solve the mystery of this unknown relative for his mother, who never knew her father, and was no longer with us.

My quest to find the identity of this man began.

My husband has wonderful memories of his Grandma A, spending time with her growing up. She was charismatic, independent and a lot of fun. She never drove, walking everywhere she went. On one occasion, she arranged a bus trip to the Minnesota State Fair. A memory he still fondly recalls.

It was an easy discovery to find Grandma A was twenty-eight years old when she had her only daughter, my husband's mother. According to multiple census', she continued living with her parents in her childhood home, even after their deaths, until marrying later in life.

Continuing my search, I uncovered a document that recorded a father's name attached to my mother-in-law. It was the only record I found, but I finally had a name.

I convinced my husband to take a DNA test to confirm what I thought was true. When the results came back, the story began to unfold.

His DNA matched others in the database; first and second cousins he was unaware of. The common denominator came back to one man, my husband's grandfather.

I reached out and learned these cousins were trying to prove their own genealogy. As adults, they heard rumors that the grandfather they grew up knowing and loving, may not be who they believed he was. Once their mother passed, they wanted to see if those rumors were true.

The DNA verified the grandfather known to them in their youth was not a blood relative. Instead, it linked them to their grandfather's friend and business partner, someone they knew and loved, never realizing he was their true grandfather.

It is my understanding this man was kind and gentle. He was a veteran in both World Wars, and served his community over the years. He never married, caring for his mother until her death. He became a boarder in his own daughter's house, though she never knew him as her father. Neither did her brother. The DNA proving, they both are half siblings of my husband's mother.

The discovery was something beyond my wildest imagination. It inspired me to write *Anneliese*, a story about Grandma A, a woman I never met, but by the stories I'm told, find to be a fascinating woman. *Dear Father* is the sequel, taking us on her daughter's journey, trying to discover her father's identity.

Please keep in mind these are fictional novels based on the few facts learned in my research. However, both novels have real life events woven into them.

The truth surrounding the circumstances discovered will never be known. The people no longer here to tell their story. What we know is the name of a man who fathered three children without ever claiming them as his. It's an intriguing, but sad story.

Just like Betz, I romanticized about what kind of man my husband's grandfather was.

Was this a love story beyond our imaginations or rather a story where promises and family secrets became more important than those it hurt?

A promise is a promise…until it's not.

About the Author

As a young child growing up in the country, Dee Miller became an avid reader. She enjoyed writing poetry and short stories during high school, never imagining one day she'd write a novel.

Her career as a historical fiction writer began after discovering intriguing facts about her husband's family tree, inspiring her to write her debut book, *Anneliese*. A fictional story based on real-life circumstances uncovered during her research. Dee began writing *Dear Father,* the sequel to *Anneliese* after receiving feedback from her readers urging her to reveal the ending to this family saga.

Dee earned her Bachelor's degree in Health Administration after she became an empty nester. She is currently retired, living in a small Midwestern town with her husband. She has two wonderful sons and five grandchildren whom she couldn't be prouder of.